The A

Wherever
You Go,
There You Are

Stephanie Schwartz

Contents

PART THREE

Wherever You Go, There You Are

— AMISH PROVERB

Your writing voice is the deepest possible reflection of who you are. The job of your voice is not to seduce or flatter or make well-shaped sentences. In your voice, your readers should be able to hear the contents of your mind, your heart, and your soul.

— MEG ROSOFF

THE GLOSSARY*

Ach! – Plain expression meaning "Oh!"

Abbeditlilch – Pennsylvania Dutch dialect word meaning "delicious."

Amische – Pennsylvania Dutch dialect word meaning "The Amish."

Baremlich – Pennsylvania Dutch dialect word meaning "terrible/horrible."

Bobbel – Pennsylvania Dutch dialect word meaning "baby" singular.

Bobbeli – Pennsylvania Dutch dialect word meaning "babies" plural.

Brode – Pennsylvania Dutch dialect word meaning "bread."

Brot – Pennsylvania Dutch dialect word meaning "proud."

Bruder – Pennsylvania Dutch dialect word meaning "brother."

Buwe – Pennsylvania Dutch dialect word meaning "boys."

Chust – Pennsylvania Dutch dialect word meaning "just."

Dat – Pennsylvania Dutch dialect word referring to or addressing one's father.

Dawdi haus – Pennsylvania Dutch dialect word meaning "a grandparents' apartment usually attached to a main house."

Denki – Pennsylvania Dutch dialect word meaning "thank you."

Ditchly – Pennsylvania Dutch dialect word meaning "bandana or work scarf."

Doddy – Pennsylvania Dutch dialect word meaning or when addressing one's "Grandfather."

Deutch – Pennsylvania Dutch word shortened from "Pennsylvania Dutch."

Englische (ers) – Pennsylvania Dutch dialect general term meaning "non-Amish."

Fa-rechth – Pennsylvania Dutch dialect word meaning "crazy."

Erschtaunlich – Pennsylvania Dutch dialect word meaning "astonishing."

Ferhoodled – Pennsylvania Dutch dialect word meaning "mixed up or newfangled."

Frau(s) – Pennsylvania Dutch dialect word meaning "wife/wives, (plural)."

Frolic(s) – Pennsylvania Dutch term for a "scheduled gathering with a single purpose in mind."

Gut – Pennsylvania Dutch dialect word meaning "good."

Gott – Pennsylvania Dutch dialect word meaning "God."

Grossmammi – Pennsylvania Dutch dialect word meaning or addressing one's "Grandmother."

Halsband – Pennsylvania Dutch dialect word meaning "husband."

Hinklehaus – Pennsylvania Dutch dialect word meaning "chicken house."

Huddlich – Pennsylvania Dutch dialect word meaning "a mess."

Kaffi – Pennsylvania Dutch dialect word meaning "coffee."

Kapp – Pennsylvania Dutch dialect word meaning "prayer cap/bonnet."

Kavli – Pennsylvania Dutch dialect word meaning "Amish double-handled diaper basket."

Kesselhaus – Pennsylvania Dutch dialect word meaning "wash house."

Kinner – Pennsylvania Dutch dialect word meaning "children."

Klimbim – German expression meaning, "junk, stuff, rubbish."

Kumm – Pennsylvania Dutch dialect word meaning "come."

Leute – German phrase meaning 'the People' or here, all "*Amische* people."

Liebling – Pennsylvania Dutch dialect word meaning "darling."

Liebesbrief – Pennsylvania Dutch dialect word meaning "love letter."

Mamm – Pennsylvania Dutch dialect word meaning "mother," or "mom."

Mammi – Pennsylvania Dutch dialect word meaning "Grandma" (familiar).

Maidel – Pennsylvania Dutch dialect word meaning "old maid."

Maud – Pennsylvania Dutch dialect word meaning "maid" usually hired.

Meedel – Pennsylvania Dutch dialect word meaning "little girl(s)."

Mitt milch – German dialect phrase meaning "with milk."

Mosch – Pennsylvania Dutch word meaning "mush" as in cornmeal cereal.

Ordnung – Plain word used by both Hutterites, Amish and Mennonites meaning "the written and unwritten rules and traditions of the Plain communities."

Redded – Pennsylvania Dutch dialect word meaning "ready/readied."

Rivvels – Pennsylvania Dutch dialect word meaning "finely grated noodle dough dumplings."

Rumschpringe – Pennsylvania Dutch dialect word meaning "running around time allowed Amish youth before joining church."

Schnitz – Pennsylvania Dutch dialect word meaning "dried apples."

Schveshta – Pennsylvania Dutch dialect word meaning "sister."

Sits ana – Pennsylvania Dutch dialect phrase meaning "(please) sit down."

Shmunzling – Pennsylvania Dutch dialect word meaning "hugging and kissing."

Wunderbar-gut – Pennsylvania Dutch dialect word meaning "wonderful and good."

Ya – Pennsylvania Dutch dialect word meaning "yes."

Youngie – Pennsylvania Dutch dialect word meaning "the youth."

Zupha – Pennsylvania Dutch dialect name of "Amish-Swiss dinner rolls."

Ztzvilling – Pennsylvania Dutch dialect word meaning "twins."

Although I have tried to represent Pennsylvania Dutch and local dialects throughout my books as accurately as I can, I am sure my readers who are native speakers will always be able to find fault for which I sincerely ask forgiveness. I know I will never get it perfect, but I hope you will allow for this. Thank you! ~ Stephanie

Part One

"*If you wish to be happy, we'll tell you the way. Don't live tomorrow till you've lived today.*"

— AMISH PROVERB

CHAPTER 1

The Letter

The house was tidy. It was immaculate, to tell the truth. It had to be. This new venture was beyond anything in Veronica's wildest dreams. A suitor, no less, not that she wanted one. She had tried her darndest to dissuade him for months. Yes, she had tried. Valiantly. Every trick in the book that she could think of actually. All her worst qualities, faults, vices, and shortcomings had been listed, plus a few extra thrown in for good measure. But he would not budge.

Veronica surveyed the kitchen. Sunshine poured through the open windows and a soft breeze rippled the blue curtains. A crisp blue checkered tablecloth covered the old oak table. Lilacs spilled over the rim of the blue-green antique Mason jar in the center of the table. A basket of fragrant rolls next to the flowers was sitting by a small crock of fresh butter with a butter knife standing upright in the center. A cut glass dish sat close by filled with thick spicy apple butter.

Across from the right side of the table was the wood stove. *How many meals have I made on that old black iron work-*

horse? A thousand? Ten thousand? she silently wondered. A gray stoneware jar sat on the top of the stove's warming oven, the sourdough starter bubbling away out of any drafts. A blue enameled covered Dutch oven was sitting toward the back of the stovetop, the potato soup with *rivvels* on a low simmer now that the coals in the firebox had died down. Her attention was drawn to the steaming brownbag apple pie sitting on a quilted hot pad on the dry sink, to cool, its fragrance ever so slightly permeating the air.

Why forever now? Veronica thought to herself as she stood barefoot, leaning against the kitchen doorway, scanning the room once again to see if she'd missed anything. Her plum-colored dress washed only yesterday was certainly flattering, though it spoke of conservatism. Gentle pleats on the sleeve caps and matching cape, not too fitted, did not deter one from thinking this is a modest woman, dressed as Amish women have dressed for scores of years. Her *kapp* was already pinned in place over her thick auburn hairs pulled tight into a low bun at the back of her neck, should her company arrive at any time; a spritz of hairspray ensuring every one of her hairs would remain in place.

I am thirty-five years old, for goodness' sake. It's hard to believe that I once had everything I'd always wanted or prayed for or wished for, chust a mere seven years ago now. Maybe I wasn't grateful enough, took Gott's *blessings for granted. I* chust *don't understand....*

Perhaps there was nothing to understand. Life throws all sorts of things our way, most unexpected. It *is* unfair. Much of life appears unfair, but then we have our families and our church to see us through. Some say "you want to make *Gott* laugh? You tell Him your plans."

Ya right, Veronica agreed with her thoughts on the subject. She headed for the back door and decided to sit on the porch swing for a spell while she waited.

She looked out over the yard. A few items flapped on the lines there, the wet sheets snapping back at the wind could be heard from where she was sitting. The vegetable garden just about ready to start harvesting. The first radishes were peeking up out of the soil; carrots and lettuce not far behind. She'd set out the little seedlings for the rest of it only two weeks ago and they were looking quite hearty already. Delicate flower buds were just popping out on the green bean bushes. Tiny soft pink flowers on the pea pod vines nodded as if in agreement with the breeze on their trellis. Even little baby eggplants appearing to look up at the sun, though soon enough they'd be too heavy and hang straight back down growing fat and turning a shiny dark purple, almost black. Honeybees were frantically trying to pollinate it all in time while the buds were just opening, but before they'd wilt and fall off.

Just then she remembered her little inspirational calendar that always sat on her dresser. Some pithy quote for each day of the year. It offered a moment of reflection before the busy day began. This morning was no different. Its message for the day was puzzling, though. Perhaps it really was meant just for her. Just for today.

"We fear the future. We fear illness and the loss of security. We fear what people may say. We fear being different from the 'herd.' We walk the earth in fear! Needless fears keep us from living a full life in Christ."

It was for sure one to ponder. She would remember it several more times that day.

The grass needed mowing. Time to move their picket and put the two sheep on this side of the house. From the huge maple in the center of the yard still hung the tire swing. Amos had put it up seven years ago now. She hadn't the heart to take it down in all this time. Her thoughts wandered then.

We were blissfully happy, she thought to herself as she swung her feet back and forth, wondering again at life's mysteries. *Getting to know each other, going to singings in barns all over the district, taking out the sleigh and the horses in winter, gallivanting to wherever we got an invitation from friends. Fixing up his courting buggy. I'd sewn the fancy purple velvet upholstery for the bench while he installed the battery headlights and a few other bells and whistles.* During *rumschpringe,* that time for 'running around' before joining church, *youngie* are allowed a few slips as far as the *Ordnung* is concerned, sort of like the grownups looking the other way, turning a blind eye. They certainly remember their own *rumschpringe* time, for sure.

Her thoughts continued as the swing rocked, back and forth, squeaking each time on its way back. *A whole year we dated, together every minute we could manage. That summer I'd pack a picnic and Amos'd pick me up and we'd go to some deserted lake and swim in our clothes. They'd dry out still on our bodies by later in the day. It was such a* wunderbar-gut *time.* Mamm *would even bake some Whoopie pies to add to the basket, and all sorts. She made them all, those yummy gigantic cream-filled cookies. Pumpkin, oatmeal, chocolate, peppermint, peanut butter, or spice.*

Although today Whoopie pies are closely associated with the Amish, their actual origins are in some dispute. Some say they came from Maine. Others that they were always a Pennsylvania Dutch invention. The name is supposed to have come from some little boy or girl discovering one in his or her lunch pail one day at school and shouting, "Whoopie!"

The letter had arrived months ago now, close to a year, truth be told. Hand addressed. Return address Canada. *Who do I know in Canada?* Veronica had asked herself at the time. Closing the mailbox, she brought the letter up to the front steps of the porch that wrapped itself around the whole house. Settling on the worn wooden top step with its pealing gray paint, she ripped open the letter.

> *Dear Veronica,*
>
> > *Greetings in our dear Lord's Name!*
>
> > *It's still chilly up here at night, but the wind is feeling warmer, promising spring is on the way.*
>
> > *It's almost lambing season and we've already had two calves born. In a hurry they were, I guess. We'll be seeing the last of the snow any day now.*
>
> > *Our bishop is related to the minister down near your district and came to see me a few weeks ago. He told me about the buggy accident your* halsband *had a few years back. First, I want to express my deepest sympathy to you. I know what you must be going through. I lost my own* frau *a little over three years ago now. You really never get over something like that, eh?*

Veronica stopped reading and looked at the return address again. *Henry Eicher. Milverton, Ontario,* she read. *Humph. No idea where that is,* she told herself. She focused back on the letter again.

> > *So, this bishop suggests I write to you. Get to know each other. Who knows what* Gott *might have planned?*

Shaking her head, Veronica lay the letter down in her lap. Looking across the yard she noted that the sheep had cleaned off the grass and weeds from the north side of the house. *Time to move their picket lines,* she mused to herself. Picking up the letter once more she read on.

I am as clueless about all this as you probably are, but I am willing to consider meeting others again. I'm not a spring chicken for sure. I am forty years old. Not much to look at, either. I have a farm here that my bruder *and I work. His family are in the big house now, and me and Rose are in the* dawdi haus. *Rose is almost three. Her* mamm *died from complications after giving birth to her. You are never prepared for something like that, eh? My parents helped me raise her as long as they were both around, and my* bruder's *family helps out now too.*

Veronica again put down the letter to think. *Hm. So, does he* chust *want a* mamm *for his* kinner, *and a cook and housekeeper, or is he looking for a wife? Big difference there, buddy,* she told herself. *Boy am I cynical today,* she chided herself. She finished reading the letter and carefully folded it up as she went back through the house, tossing it on the table. Stopping dead in her tracks at the bottom of the stairs she looked back at the letter where she'd left it. Then looking back at the wood stove, she pondered tossing it into the wood box there. *Problem solved,* she told herself. *Maybe later when I make supper.*

CHAPTER 2
A Marriage of Convenience

Veronica spent the next two days going around in circles in her head after receiving the letter. Should she reply? What would she say? She knew such things were done, 'a marriage of convenience' it was often called. He'll run the farm and she'll keep things going smoothly in the house. But was love ever a part of the equation? Could one learn to love under such an arrangement? What if you just weren't suited? Did you simply resign yourself for the rest of your life while trying to convince yourself that it was *Gott's* will? Could you then spend years living a joyless existence? It was hard to imagine. She didn't feel trapped in her unfortunate life but could certainly see how some poor widow might think that and end up agreeing to it.

Enough *schveshtas* had tried their hand at matchmaking. It was relentless. This one or that one trying to get her hitched. Making matches with their bachelor brother or widowed cousin or some other poor unmarried fellow off in another *Amische* settlement they'd heard of. All of a sudden half the Amish world had unmarried *bruders* outnumbering *schveshtas,* according to these women. They were on a crusade, it appeared.

Clara, another *frau* in the local district, literally accosted Veronica one church Sunday as they were *redding* the buffet after the service. It was too cold in the barn to hold lunch there afterwards so while the large rooms in the house were fitted out by the men present with tables, benches and chairs for the meal, knocking about, bumping into each other, clattering the benches into place, trying their darndest to puzzle as many tables into the space as would be possible, Clara had sidled up to Veronica in the kitchen. The women were just as jostled about trying to fit into the kitchen, as large as it was, but hurrying to get the dishes lined up for lunch. Clara literally bumped into Veronica, though later Veronica wondered if it had been calculated to create a ruse so she could speak to her.

"Oops! Soft landing, so very sorry, Veronica," Clara said, putting on her sweetest smile. "Do excuse me, Veronica."

"No problem," Veronica replied as she continued slicing a block of cheese.

"I was hoping to bump into you, (chuckle) no pun intended," Clara forged on. "But I have been meaning to tell you about Steven Lapp. His *frau* left him about two years ago —do you remember—over in Michigan, you might have heard about it. Well, it turns out she died in a car crash a while back here now. So unfortunate. She'd gone *Englische.* She'd always seemed so unhappy with everything, never satisfied with our Plain life. Anyway, she'd been out drinking and partying, they say."

"No, I hadn't heard. That's terrible. Awful. Such a waste.

Poor man," Veronica said, sincerely expressing her empathy. "Did she leave any *kinner?*"

"No, but then I heard tell she didn't really want them. Can you imagine?" Clara gossiped on. "But he's really nice. A distant cousin to me. You could always write to him. He'd be a real *gut* catch...."

"Um, Clara," Veronica cut her off. "I am not interested in marrying again. Thank you for caring, though."

"Well, you know you should consider it. You are still young. He needs a *gut* faithful *frau*—" Clara insisted.

"I am sure he does, but I am not available. Case closed," Veronica said turning around to finish layering cheese slices onto a large platter.

"But you can't *chust* put it off forever, dear," Clara forged on, becoming downright aggressive, if not utterly obnoxious. She had convinced herself that it was her express mission in life to get Veronica a husband. And sooner than later.

"Yes, I can. Please understand," Veronica tried to reason with her.

"You *chust* won't listen to sense. I've tried to help you, to be a *gut* friend. You know that," Clara persisted.

"I know, but I will ask you *when* and *if* I am ever ready, okay?" Veronica pleaded.

"But I've told you this over and over and you won't let us help you. If I have to tell you again," Clara sputtered, "if I have to tell you one more time... I...I... I WILL!" she practically shouted and quickly stalked off in a huff.

"Uh-huh," Veronica agreed under her breath. *And I am never going to, Clara,* Veronica thought to herself as she picked up the platter and headed toward the buffet table.

She decided to try to write back anyway. She told herself she would try—that didn't mean she'd actually send it, though. This was definitely the most preposterous twist so far that life had offered her. As unexpected as a buggy accident....

Dear Henry,

Greetings in our dear Lord's Holy Name!

Thank you for your letter. It was quite a surprise if I am honest. I am not young anymore either. I am chust *a plain old* Amische frau *trying to make sense of the world I presently find myself in while hoping I don't become a heretic in the process. I confess I am a bit of a philosopher. I was a schoolteacher and assumed I would do that my whole life. I would have been happy doing that, don't ya know? But life never turns out how you planned, eh? "Tell* Gott *your plans and make Him laugh"—I know. I know I shouldn't doubt; I know He will care for me, and I needn't worry. But—and there is always that 'but,' eh? But how can I* chust *accept it all without understanding anything?* Chust *trust you say. Yes, I know. I've heard that too. Some say, 'faith is higher than reason.' Others spout, 'worry ends where faith begins.' I try. I do. I want to. But....*

You'd do far better finding some young starry-eyed maidel. *I can't imagine getting to know someone all over again. I know I'm rambling here, but I often write down my thoughts. Sometimes I don't know what I'm thinking till I write it all down. Silly of me, I know. It all started with a diary I was given one Christmas when I was little. How I loved that diary with its gold clasp and tiny key! I hugged it to my chest and actually cried when I thanked* Mamm *and* Dat. *Usually we only got a new tin mug with an orange, and some peppermint sticks in it—chust like Laura and Mary back in the* Little House on the Prairie *books. We felt so very special. I still have my little blue speckled enamel mug. Over the next few years this obsession turned into the horde in my bottom drawer, full of diaries, sometimes more than one a year. Now my writing fills whole notebooks. I suppose I could burn them all some-day...they would make great tinder for the wood stove. I should. They aren't much use to anyone really.* Chust *my ramblings, again. The only audience I write for is myself and the Lord, of course, though He can read my heart anytime He wants to, which I am sure He does, though He has far more important things to do than hang around the likes of me. No one else will ever read it all. Downright boring.*

Yes, I am trying to dissuade you. You should put all this out of your head. I guess you should ask the bishop for some other leads. I believe Gott *has already picked out the perfect* frau *for you. I assure you of my prayers for you and little Rose.*

Friend Veronica

...and it ain't me, she told herself as she folded up the letter.

A little over two weeks later another letter arrived in the mailbox. Veronica was on her knees, hunched over in the garden pulling weeds when the mailman's little white truck drove up to the end of her driveway. Standing up, stretching her arms, and scrunching her shoulders felt good. It was getting too warm to be out in the sun for much longer anyway. *Lunchtime,* she told herself. She walked down to the mailbox while dusting her hands off on her old, gray twill apron, and pulled out the bundle there. Farm catalogs she'd never cancelled but should have long ago, flyers for the town's local firemen's pancake breakfast fundraiser, Lehman's Non-electric catalog, Gohn Brothers' latest edition of their little dry goods newsletter from Middlebury, Indiana, then a copy of *Family Life* magazine, and the larger copy of *The Budget,* the Amish-Mennonite weekly newspaper that keeps the Plain churches throughout North America informed of all the goings-on in all the settlements. It is second best when not having telephones at home.

And then there was the letter that she'd dreaded. *Surely my last letter should have completely ended the whole affair.* She turned the envelope over and checked the return address. *Yup, it's Henry,* she confirmed. *Not that it was even an affair,* she reminded herself, sarcastically. *I never should have sent it at all in the first place. Let it die a natural death is what I should've done. Whatever now?* She wearily slammed the mailbox door shut with a bang and turned toward the house.

Listen, fella, she continued to herself as she trudged up the drive. *I thought I was clear. Crystal clear. No, I do not want to get to know you, or any other widower for that matter. End of discussion,* she chided herself. But she didn't end it there. Her thoughts continued to bombard her. *Couldn't the bishop up there find him a wife in all of Canada? Is he that needy? Or is he simple or something? Why are they trying to foist him on me? They don't know a thing about me, for pity's sake!*

She shuffled up the incline to the kitchen door and went in, scraping her bare feet several times on the jute rug there while still frowning her disapproval. Bending over she picked out a weed stuck between two toes and threw it back outside. She removed the sweaty *ditchly* from her head and tossed it into the wicker laundry basket sitting on the floor in the entry. Dropping the stack of mail on the table she went to the sink and opened the spigot on the gravity water tank filling the basin there. Her homemade lavender soap smelled wonderful as she scrubbed her nails with the little brush in the water. Lavender always had a way of relaxing you. *I have to make more soap to bring when we go to that Sunrise store again. It sure sells* gut *there,* she reminded herself, *making a mental note.*

She poured lemonade into her oversize coffee mug still

sitting by the sink from earlier that morning and brought it over to the table. Taking a deep breath, she sat down and proceeded to open the letter. Then she stopped. *Maybe I should* chust *burn it without even reading it. That'd put an end to this nonsense,* she told herself. Taking a large swig of the lemonade she stood up and grabbed the iron handle used to lift the individual round iron plates on the wood stove over the firebox. She clicked it into the indented hook on the frontmost iron plate on the stove top, lifted the plate up, and held the letter over the hole while looking down into the smoldering coals there.

CHAPTER 3

Henry Eicher

A s of 2016 there were twenty-one different Canadian Amish settlements mostly scattered throughout southern Ontario. The largest Amish settlement in Canada is in the Milverton area. When the Amish first came from Europe to the Waterloo Region in 1823, they settled west of Kitchener and then spread out from there. By 1874 they were moving into Mornington Township, where Milverton is located. When some Amish began building meetinghouses in the 1880s, the Amish of the Milverton area did not all agree on such a radical move, resulting in a split. The progressives proceeded to build meetinghouses then, and eventually referred to themselves as "Mennonite," while the traditionalists are the people we now refer to as the "Amish" today and still continue to meet in their homes, taking turns throughout the year to host church there.

Henry Eicher was tending to the evening milking in the expansive barn. There was plenty of straw for the cows in each stall and loads of grain and hay in their feed boxes. The twenty cows had come in from the field as it became dusk. They had come in at this time every day of their lives thus far and knew the drill without being called. They would be grateful to be relieved of their milk besides. Above them from the rafters hung three Coleman lanterns, the only light illuminating the barn. The corners of the room were swathed in shadows. The heat from the bovine bodies rose up in little clouds of fog as did their breaths. The long cement slab down the middle of the two rows of cow stanchions hadn't been swept yet after the cows had come in dragging every kind of debris from the field. A few cow pies littered the path besides. Henry would have to come back in before he went to bed and sweep it clean. Not the time to be lazy if you're trying to run a farm.

The unadorned windows lining both outer walls reflected the dim light proving that night was indeed quickly descending. It was silent in the old bank barn save for an occasional nicker from one of the horses or the tiny mews from the new litter of kittens up in the hay mow.

Got to bring Rosie up to see those cats tomorrow. She'll love that, Henry told himself.

Henry and his brother didn't have any of the modern milking equipment that some Amish have adopted. He was still doing it all the old-fashioned way: by hand, moving the little three-legged stool from one cow to the next, positioning it either to her right or left, and then sanitizing each teat protruding from the expanded udder bag with rags soaked in disinfectant sodium hypochlorite solution from a clean bucket. A second sterile bucket was then switched in and he could milk each teat until the udder appeared stripped of its contents before moving on to the next cow. The *ker-ping ker-ping* of the milk hitting the sides of the galvanized pails always had a calming effect on him. He was able to block out all the worries of the day, and let this moment lull him into feeling only peace. Peace with his world in this little patch of God's green earth. Peace in spite of all that had happened, that appeared to upend everything he thought he understood and believed in.

He'd hung his straw hat up by the door so he could see what he was doing better. His fraying straw hat had matted down his hairs and left them sticking to his sweaty forehead. A hair cut was about three months overdue. His black homemade quilted vest was badly in need of a wash. So were the black denim barndoor trousers, too. He hardly noticed the odor of sweat on his three-day old shirt. Without a wife around these things easily got neglected. He marveled every day now at all the things she had done around the house and farm that he hadn't ever taken notice of before, had taken for granted. And now she was gone. Taking a deep breath, he settled down by the first cow and wringing out the cloth in the solution began wiping down the udder, something he had been doing for over three decades now, twice a day, every day, since he was just a little wood chopper, barely ten years old. But his mind was not in that barn this time. It was thousands of miles away wondering about Veronica. What did she look like? How progressive was their church? How many *kinner* did she have? Her letter in reply to his first letter didn't say much at all except that she was clearly not interested. She thought she had closed the subject after sending it, though Henry was anything but dissuaded. He was actually encouraged. My, but they had a lot of things in common! It was startling, actually.

Well, Gott, Henry's thoughts began, *maybe you really do have a hand in all this after all and it isn't* chust *a random act on the part of the bishop.* Chust *maybe You have something* wunderbar *in store for both of us. I don't know how I can convince her, though. She for sure sounds like she knows her own mind and isn't afraid to speak it either. Maybe she is feisty or* chust *has a chip on her shoulder. Maybe all the hardship has made her bitter. It does do for some. But boy, I for certain would like to meet her. Wonder what she looks like? Tall or blonde or little or stout?* Henry's mind went to the ornate, little maple cutting board hanging in his kitchen that had been a wedding gift only four years ago now. It said, "A plump wife and a big barn never did any man harm." *Well now then,* Gott, he mused and chuckled to himself. *I have the big barn. Now You* chust *have to supply the* frau. He chuckled again and shook his head. *I suppose I'm no longer considered a* gut *catch though. At my age, and with a* bobbel, *and I'm nothing special to look at either. Maybe she thinks I am needy or lost a few marbles myself after all we went through. Maybe she doesn't want to take on something she hasn't a clue about. Remarriage isn't for everyone. We aren't giddy* youngie *anymore. It was for sure different when you live in the same community and practically grew up together, knowing each other's families. Gosh, what do I write back? I need some help here, Lord. This for certain is new territory for me. I need some inspiration, please.* He stood up, and grabbing the full milk bucket with one hand slapped the jet-black cow's side to let her know he was finished.

"Well, there, Espresso," he said out loud. "You got any bright ideas on the subject? I could sure use some help here." He brought the milk pail to the dairy room then, away from the dust and flies in the barn. He would strain them all together later when he was done. Grabbing another clean bucket, he proceeded to the next cow and sat down.

"Well, hullo there Barak," he began, addressing the huge black beauty he'd named after the famous president he'd followed in the papers, as he washed her off. "What is your opinion on the subject? Any wisdom? No? Maybe a tad? Not really? I need all the help I can get. I guess I'll pray on it some and try to put together a letter later tonight when the *bobbel* is asleep. Yup. Maybe I'll get some wisdom between now and then," he said as he swiped his arm across his moist forehead. *I sure hope so,* he told himself. At the time he was living with his brother and sister-in-law where Rose had been added to the herd of *kinner* there. "Free-range *kinner,*" his *bruder* called them.

CHAPTER 4
Halloween Soup

Veronica finished eating her supper and wiped out the soup bowl with a thick slice of bread that she then ate. 'Bird seed bread' is what she and her brothers and sisters called it growing up because of all the millet, poppy seeds, sunflower seeds, and sesame seeds in it. Amos had liked this soup so very much, Sunshine Squash Soup. As children they called it Halloween soup because it was so orange, even though they didn't celebrate the pagan holiday, but they couldn't completely ignore it, what with all the *Englischers* buying up every last pumpkin from every single *Amishche* farm growing them in the entire county every year, and in spite of expanding the crop year after year. With ingredients like pumpkin or butternut squash, carrots, rutabaga, yams, and curry it couldn't *not* be Halloween soup. She liked to start with chicken broth left over from boiling the 'spent hens,' those old gals who had stopped laying. They could still make a good soup if boiled long enough.

The air in the kitchen was turning chilly with dusk settling in. Veronica closed the windows and pulled the *Ordnung*-prescribed green shades down. Pouring a large mug of decaf coffee from the pot on the wood stove, she quickly washed up her dishes and set them on a towel on the dry sink to air, the whole time thinking about what to write next. Maybe put down some thoughts in her journal, just to sort of formulate her next 'plan of attack,' so to speak.

Her letter to Henry had the opposite effect from what she had hoped for. She was convinced that it would surely put an end to the whole thing, that she could get back to her everyday, if not dull life. This whole thing was consuming her thoughts day and night, in the garden, in the barn, in bed at night. How was she to rid herself of this pest, as she was now referring to him? He would not be easily dissuaded. She would just have to try even harder.

Veronica looked through the wood box until she found the right size log there and opening the firebox on the stove, shoved it in over the coals, slamming the little door shut. *That should keep until morning,* she told herself as she turned the metal crank on the damper in the stovepipe to close it for the night. On her way up to bed she remembered another confrontation after church earlier in the day, but this was a far more pleasant one. Much more indeed.

Ruby Schmucker had spied Veronica in the parking lot that day (for the buggies, bikes and scooters) as they left church at the Lehman's farm. She was as sweet as ever. Dear Ruby. They had gone through all eight grades together, mixed up in all the same mischief all those years ago. The two of them hiding, up on the outhouse roof during recess one time. If you lay flat on your stomach, no one could see you up there because the tarpapered roof tilted up facing the school-house. They thought they'd make Teacher find them, but she never came. She'd let them down, outwitted them for sure, that being the case. They'd stayed up there a good long while after hearing the bell heralding that recess was over. When Pauline Yoder came out to use the outhouse at one point, they'd even talked her into climbing up there with them.

Eventually they got bored and climbed back down the makeshift stairs they'd made from the apple crates littering the ground. Next to the outhouse was the little lean-to that housed Teacher's horse in bad weather. They sat on a hay bale playing Cat's Cradle for a while until they heard a faint noise. Upon investigation, the now-three little girls discovered the black cat that called the shack its home. She'd had a litter hiding behind the stack of hay bales there. Most of the afternoon was then spent petting the darling little kittens. Veronica still thought the memory of that day was worth the consequences that followed, though she wagered she probably wouldn't do it again at the time.

"Is it ever *gut* to see you!" Ruby said, running up to Veronica in the parking lot, apparently oblivious to the fact that she was most obviously 'in the family way.'

"Oh, Ruby! Don't run. How are you? I didn't know…when is it *k…kumming?* Looks like any day now if you ask me." Veronica stammered.

"But I didn't ask you, missy," Ruby frowned and attempted to feign offence. "Time will tell," Ruby answered with a chuckle. "No *Amische mamm* will tell you that. Anyway, *bobbeli kumm* when they're ready. I never put any stock in due dates. They're always wrong and you get all anxious, thinking it's too early, or too late and you'll never have it." Ruby laughed, sliding her arm into Veronica's.

"I was hoping to bump into you…." Ruby giggled at the pun. It took Veronica another minute to get the joke and groan.

"You're naughty! You were always the funny one. How are you? How many is it now?" Veronica wanted to know.

"This one will be six. They keep getting cuter, *ya* know. I adore every one of them," Ruby said.

"Well, you must. Let me *kumm* help you, would *ya? Chust* for a few days after this one? We could catch up on old times. Wouldn't that be fun?" Veronica asked.

"It would be *wunderbar. Ya.* I'd like that. A million thanks! Gee, I can't wait now. By the way, any nibbles in the *halsband* department?" Ruby asked, taking Veronica's hand.

"Boy, have I got the stories for *ya,*" Veronica said shaking her head as they walked toward the buggies.

"But any *gut* prospects yet?" Ruby wanted to know.

"Well, maybe one. Time will tell," she chuckled. "But you'd think every *frau* in the district was now an official matchmaker. It's *ferhoodled.* I feel like I'm being stalked. Wherever I go there's some *mamm* or *mammi* with the latest news report on available widowers and bachelors. It is nuts, is what it is. Quilting bees are the worst. Baby showers. I've *chust* stopped going. And the apple butter frolic over at the Glicks' last week, my but what a circus."

The fact was that Ruby was Veronica's oldest and dearest friend. She could tell her anything. There was no one else to confide in. Amos was gone now. Her own *mamm,* too. She knew her sisters were terrible gossips, though they'd each deny the fact to the hilt if confronted about it. She couldn't trust them with such special news, and she didn't want the entire community privy to the state of her love life, even if it wasn't exactly that, quite yet. She knew her *schveshtas* meant well and had her best interest in mind, but you'd think they'd been assigned by some divine edict that it was their life's work to procure a husband for their sister. Never mind she had repeatedly made it clear she was not interested, and probably never would be. Apparently, they ignored her protests, deciding they knew best.

"We'll have the whole time I'm being your *bobbel maud* to

catch up. It'll be such fun," Veronica said, squeezing Ruby's arm closer.

She'd started another journal earlier in the year, mostly to put down her thoughts, but partly with the idea of someday writing a novel. Not that she had any story line or plot thought out, but if others could write so many *wunderbar* books from their Amish communities, maybe she could, too. She didn't think she had enough imagination to be a proper writer, but it was fun to fantasize. After the supper dishes were dispatched, she ran up the stairs to her bedroom and grabbed the speckled black and white composition notebook and the jar of pencils she kept on top of her dresser.

She stopped then and glanced at the little stand-up inspirational calendar she'd set there. It often had such amazing words of wisdom that she thought it could have been written expressly for her. Today was no different.

"God speaks quietly, very quietly but He does speak, and He will make known to you what He wants you to do."

"Well, Catherine. You've done it again. Food for thought for sure. *Please, Lord, help me to listen to you,* Veronica prayed as she walked back downstairs.

Returning to the kitchen she carefully placed each item on the table and surveyed the setting there. Grabbing the pencils, she walked barefoot over to the sideboard and sharpened all of them in the antique metal pencil sharpener that was screwed down in place on the edge of the wooden countertop, quickly turning the handle around and around until each had a perfectly sharp point. Sitting down she opened the notebook and read what she had written Sunday before last.

So, this is my story. It doesn't have an ending. Not yet. I will have to add that on later, perhaps in another journal. I don't know what will happen next, but I must write it all down.

I guess I should start at the beginning. That would make more sense, I suppose. Well, let's see. Okay. Here goes nothing.

She stopped to erase the last four lines. Those were just superfluous words. Not needed. She'd never forgotten the *Little House* books her *dat* read to them every night at bedtime. When he'd finished the last chapter of the last book of the series, he would just start over again with the first one. She'd always wanted to emulate Laura and write like she did. Maybe she wasn't too old to do just that. She continued reading while sipping the now-tepid coffee.

CHAPTER 5

Liebesbriefs (Love Letters)

T he letter never actually got dropped into the fire. Hopelessly curious by nature, insatiably inquisitive, Veronica could not go through with it. She held it over the coals while she wrestled with wanting to and not wanting to burn it. In the end she had replaced the iron plate on the stove and squashed the envelope into her apron waist, peeved with herself for what she perceived as a serious character flaw. She angrily unhooked and then tossed the iron plate handle onto the side of the stovetop where it dropped with a clang. Couldn't she just forget it and move on? But no, she couldn't. She had not read it. She didn't want to, really didn't desire this at all, not one little bit, but then she didn't want to wonder for the rest of her life what it could possibly contain. And she knew it would haunt her forever: What was in that letter anyway?

"Darn it! Shhhhh... sugar!" she groused, hands on hips. "Surely not another *liebesbrief"* she voiced out loud as she went through the back door, egg basket in hand to feed the chickens. It always calmed her to walk through the wet morning grass with bare feet on her way to do chores. It took longer today for the feelings to settle down and find any semblance of peace. He wasn't worth it. Henry Eicher WAS...NOT...worth the frustration and agony that his letters had elicited. *He sure likes to write the love letters* she thought. She stopped halfway to the *hinklehaus* when she noticed the slugs. Great big slimy things they were, slithering in slow motion straight for her flower bed. How did the darn things know where to go? Did they have noses? Or eyes? Why did *Gott* even make them? *And* Gott, she thought to herself, chust *tell me what is it with the mosquitoes?* She mentally added the slugs to the list of questions she had amassed that she would ask Him someday, that is if she even made it into heaven. By now she'd be at grave risk of not making the grade, she figured. To get into heaven. If only she could find a way to be less negative. She knew it was her worst fault. *More of a battle is what it is,* she told herself. Then finding a large leaf nearby she picked up half a dozen of the wet brown gastropods, each one recoiling at her touch into a tight little ball and held them there on the leaf while she headed toward the driveway where the ducks always started out their day pecking through the gravel for bugs. When they saw her coming, they spread their wings, lowered their heads, and ran full tilt toward her. They knew that walk. She had treats!

She held out her hand to each of them in turn, dropping the plump delicacy onto her palm first. *Duck caviar,* she said to herself chuckling at the obvious, absolute bliss the ducks found in eating the little critters. She could never feed them enough of them.

Dear Veronica,
Greetings of Love in our Dear Lord's Name!

It is finally warming up here so we can get on with planting. It's been a late Spring in coming. We are so much farther north from you that it is often weeks later than your crops down there further south.

I was delighted to get your letter. I understand your hesitancy —I do—don't get me wrong. This kind of thing isn't taught in school. I wish it was. Like bobbeli *in a way. You wish they'd come with instructions, but they never do, eh? We don't have to rush anything though.* Chust *get to know each other 'from afar' as they say.*

That said, maybe I should tell you a bit about myself. First, I have to say I was amazed at how much we already have in common. I too was a schoolteacher. I know that is a rarity. A male teacher, in an Amische *school, eh? I went to school in a one-room schoolhouse* chust *like you, I imagine, but Canada was years behind in passing laws that the U.S. had in place already, like allowing us* Amische *to even have our own schools. My older siblings all had to go to public school before me. It was the law. We didn't have a choice, but then finally, after the parents and ministers petitioned for years, we were allowed to have our own schools, but they had to be staffed by certified teachers back then. With only an eighth-grade education, that wasn't possible for us. So, the government always hired outside teachers to run the schools in our settlements. They tended to hire Mennonites who would be more sympathetic to our ways and culture than, say,* Englischers *would be. Well then, we get word a few more years down the line that in the States the law allowed the* Amische *schools to be taught by Amish girls without any more than an eighth-grade education. Were we ever excited then! At first, when we approached the authorities, they were pretty skeptical and decided to test the prospective teachers in order to be assured that there would be some kind of standard of education, so they did that. Some qualified on the first try while others didn't. We got together then and brainstormed how we should help each other and be sure we were covering enough material so that the scholars could at least function in whatever they decided to do in life, be it farming or business or construction or shops. We knew there could be the danger of not teaching enough or ineffective teachers who had no clue what they were doing. Well, this all went on until we had a pretty sound plan in place and have been doing it ever since.*

When I was in grade school—we had our own school by then —but it was before we had our own Amish teachers and we had only the Mennonites. When I was in third grade, we had a young Mennonite frau *who, it struck me, was not unlike our own* mamms *and* schveshtas, kapps *and all. She was awfully nice, and we learned a lot. Then the following year we teamed up with a nearby district that couldn't find a teacher and got sent a Mennonite man. Boy, were my parents wary. Could he teach? Would he have the patience needed for a one-room schoolhouse with grades one through eight? He turned out to be amazing. I had the best year ever when he came. He wanted us to call him Brother Schrock or* chust *Teacher. That's when I decided I wanted to be a teacher when I grew up, more than anything else in the whole wide world.*

Well, I studied hard and never wavered from that hope. Sure, I worked hard on the farm and did everything in the barn and learned everything I'd need to know as a farmer from my dat, *but I never stopped wanting to be a teacher. And I did it. The year I turned eighteen I took the test and passed, though Brother Schrock mentored me that year and made sure I knew everything they would ask. It wasn't cheating, more like going to school again, which I loved. He was managing, but by then the school had grown and so had the adjoining district so he wrote to the board suggesting they renew his contract and take me on as a student teacher which they readily approved, and I got to teach with him three more years that way. Was I ever lucky or what? It was my dream come true. So that's what I did until* Dat *died and left me and my brother the farm. That's what I am doing now. If they ever asked me to teach again, I wouldn't hesitate for a minute. I later met two other* Amische bruders *who were teachers in Canada, too.*

Well, I figure I've rambled on here long enough. Hope I haven't put you to sleep. Please tell me more about yourself. And know I will pray to do Gott's *will and not my own in all of this as I know you will be doing too.*

Your bruder *in Christ,*
Henry

CHAPTER 6

Single Ladies

Veronica sat at the kitchen table planning her day. She'd just finished her breakfast of baked oatmeal with dried cranberries, pumpkin seeds, butter, honey and camel milk, and was jotting down the errands she needed to do and the groceries she planned to get at the Dutch Market General Store over in Shipshewana, an Amish-owned and run business being their first stop.

Hey, wait here a minute, you say. Yes, camel milk. The local health food co-op had just started stocking it after discovering Humpback Dairies in Missouri, owned and operated by an Amish-Mennonite family. Not unlike goat milk, though some say it is richer, it's also better tolerated by people with lactose intolerance. Shipshewana was too far for the horse and buggy to go, but two of her Amish girlfriends had scheduled a van trip to do the shopping that week. There were seven of them in the surrounding districts— single Amish women who frequently made an effort to get together and encourage one another. Some lived alone like Veronica. Others lived with large Amish families who had hired them to help as live-in *mauds* with all the work and *huddlich* that a family with lots of children demanded. With the Amish still having large families even today--the average between six and twelve children--the position could be a full-time job. A *mamm* having a new baby and several other young children at home would definitely welcome an extra pair of capable hands.

Too old to join the *youngie*—the young people's groups where Amish youth regularly meet to hold gatherings designed to facilitate getting to know other young people—the older single sisters found that they enjoyed each other's company and often planned get-togethers like this shopping trip today. Of course, lunch out at some roadside café would be included. They'd all chipped in to pay the van driver who was often a retired Mennonite man or woman who enjoyed the extra work. At least once a year they would visit other settlements in other states, often connecting with other single sisters' groups. Last year the *fraus* took a train all the way to Pinecraft in Florida, an Amish getaway vacation destination where many Amish people go to enjoy the sun, the beach, and a more relaxed atmosphere than some of their home districts. Instead of horses and buggies, Pinecraft is home to a fleet of motorized golfcarts and three-wheeled bikes which the Amish *grossmammis* and *doddys* can rent and quickly learn how to propel without much fuss. Canoeing, kayaking, beach combing, and picnics lure Amish from as far away as Canada each year.

Many single Amish women find like-minded sisters through newsletters now available to them. Among the numerous periodicals written and published by the Amish* for the Amish, some dating their humble beginnings as far back as the 1890s, is one little magazine called, *Single Symphony*, a quarterly magazine filled with letters from single Amish and Old Order Mennonite women of all ages.

*For a longer list see the 'Appendix' page at the end of this book.

Dutch Market popped up just a few years ago as more and more young Amish families moved to northern Minnesota, having found less and less available—or affordable—land in Wisconsin, Pennsylvania, Ohio, Michigan, and South Dakota, especially. Walking down the aisles of the large store you can find just about anything an Amish home or farm might need from handmade bird houses to bulk peanut butter, giant tubs of whipped marshmallow fluff, and lard, birthday cards, and even last-minute wedding gifts. Everyday straw hats and black Sunday hats in sizes from tiny boys to large men's hats are stacked next to a wall of horseshoes, also in a variety of sizes. Home canned jams, jellies, pickles and relishes and other canned goods line shelves from the floor up. There are bulk bags of gelatin, tapioca, rice, nuts, beans, Kool-Aid, dry yeast, potato flakes, grains, shredded coconut, chocolate chips, flours, jars of honey—just about everything is on offer. Hair clips, baby toys, fresh eggs, barn boots, clothes lines and clothes pins, canning lids and rings, spices, handkerchiefs for *dats, mamms* and children, cookbooks, and alternative vitamins and supplements for anything that ails the human race, are all there. There is a table displaying Franny's hand-dipped chocolates that she makes and sells out of her house up the road. Franny is also a member of the single *fraus'* group.

Veronica startled when there was a knock on the back door. She hadn't heard the van come up the driveway. Probably while she was doing up the dishes she figured. Quickly grabbing her stiff black travel bonnet, she carefully placed it over her white *kapp* while slipping her arm through the handles of her black leather pocketbook and called for her guest to *kumm* in.

"Are *ya redded* up?" the woman called as she stepped through the mud room.

"*Ya*, I'm here. *Gut* to see you! How long has it been?" Veronica asked as she reached her visitor.

"Only two weeks ago at church is all," her friend answered, chuckling.

"Well, it for sure seems longer!" Veronica answered laughing as she finished tying the bonnet ribbons under her chin and heartily shook hands with her friend.

"Everyone else is in the van," Ruthie reported.

"But I thought only you and Hazel were *kumming*..." she exclaimed.

"Well, we got one more at the last minute. Matilda decided to *kumm* too," Ruthie added.

"Ooooh!" Veronica replied, very pleasantly surprised by this addition. "Oh, that is *gut* news for sure! And Franny doesn't need her to make chocolates today?"

"No, Franny sends her regrets, she would have loved to *kumm* too, but she's got a large order for her chocolate pecan turtles and they made most of them yesterday, but she has to get them *redded* for mailing today still," Ruthie explained.

Ruthie and Veronica piled into the van, first greeting Mrs. Dyck, their driver for the day. Then hugs were shared all around, as much as you could manage in a vehicle before they all settled down and buckled their seatbelts for the much-anticipated outing.

"Hazel, please tell me what you're doing now," Veronica began.

"Well," she started. "You know the Lehmann's over by

the Hay River, right? Well, she *chust* had baby number nine. Healthy little dishwasher, all of ten pounds! Eats like a champ. No hairs. Because she is so big everyone thinks she's a boy. The other kids adore her, too. I don't think she gets put down once during a day. Their *mamm* sure has those *kinner* trained too, don't *ya* know? Everything from keeping the wood box by the stove full, to bathing the little ones. Keeping up with the chickens, the gardens, they even do the cooking, the older girls do. Five of them go to school so it is quieter during the day. I don't know why they even need me. Their *dat* couldn't be any more *brot* of them," she added. And then, conspiratorially, behind her hand she whispered, "she's even got the *halsband* changing diapers, don't *ya* know?"

At that the whole van erupted in howls of laughter.

"Well, that's the way to do it if you don't want to crack up with a big family like that," Hazel concluded.

"For certain," Matilda agreed. "Well, I've been up to my elbows with the chocolates. Orders *kumming* in from all over. Franny even got a table at the farmers' market and took an order for a wedding, of all things. They want chocolates on each plate at the reception. *Englischers* they are. And then she sits there and sells out every Saturday, too at the market. She's got them in little clear plastic boxes now and got labels printed. So cute. Pretty *gut* for a *grossmammi,* I'd say."

Veronica piped up then. "Did you know Rebekah Schwartz up on highway seventy has plywood signs up all over the county roads and is taking orders for her pies for Thanksgiving? She says the *Englischers* are driving up and placing orders and paying up front in cash when they order. Then she gives them a time and a date to pick up their pies and keeps track of it all. She's got pumpkin, mince, apple, coconut custard, chocolate and pecan. I told her she should add Shoo-fly pie too. They've got that new house over near Shipshewana. The front room is *chust* for the baked goods. She has regular bakery shelves and also makes *brode* and cookies and rolls, too. The room is huge with a proper counter. The bishop even approved a phone—for business purposes only, of course. They're building some kind of chicken business in back; that looks pretty big, too."

"My turn?" Ruthie laughed. The others all nodded while passing around a tin of miniature *schnitz* pies. "Well, I'm still staying in the *dawdi haus* at my brother's place. They've got a new little wood chopper, about eight months old now. Funniest little fellow. He crawls all over after the cat and started meowing too. Thinks he's a cat!" That certainly elicited the chuckles. "And she had to stay on bed rest after him, *ya* know, after five whoppers like that and she'll need some surgery to put things back, *ya* know, prolapse and all. So, I'll stay and help out. Oh! Last night I made the best dish for supper. Maudie's column had it in last week's *Budget*. It's called 'Best Ever Corn Casserole.'"

"What's in it?" Veronica wanted to know and then took a bite of her little apple *schnitz* pie while waiting for Ruthie to answer.

"Let me see," Ruthie thought. "Whole kernel canned corn, an egg, a chopped onion, a can of cream style corn, sour cream—it was eight ounces I reckon--and one package of that Jiffy corn muffin mix and dried parsley. You mix it all up in a buttered dish and bake at about 350 degrees for forty-five minutes. They for sure cleaned that one up!"

"Sounds *gut,*" Mrs. Dyck piped up from the front of the van while the others agreed with her. "You ladies are talking about all this food and it isn't even lunch time yet!" she laughed. "You're making me hungry," the plump lady said and chuckled.

"Here, take this," someone called as a little handheld, schnitz pie was handed to her over the seat.

"And what mischief have you been up to now Veronica?" Hazel queried.

"Well first I want to read something I brought along from *The Budget*. It's hysterically funny. You might have seen it already," she began. "Someone sent it in to *The Budget* saying it was from a cookbook that a kindergarten school-teacher put together down in San Marcos, Texas."

"Are there Amish there?" someone in the rear of the car wanted to know.

"I don't know," Veronica answered as she rummaged through her purse. A few seconds later Matilda spoke up.

"I do," Matilda shyly offered. Hesitating a moment, she finally shared what she knew. "I heard about them in my bird-watching club. An article in their magazine said," she quoted from memory: "The Bee County Amish settlement attracted national attention—at least in the birding community—when a rare Northern Wheatear took up residence on John Borntrager's farm last year. Birders flocked there from around the country to Texas to catch a glimpse of it. John Borntrager named it 'Wanderer.' It was quite a sensation. Wish I'd have gotten a look at it. He wrote about it in *The Budget* that year, too. It's from the Arctic. Don't know how it got that lost, though. Pretty crazy, eh?"

Veronica continued to rifle through her purse to find what she was looking for and eventually did; smoothing the paper out she began to read, already trying not to laugh: "Here it is." She read, "It's called 'Sebastian's Pancakes. Serves three people. Prep time: ten minutes. Cook time: three minutes. Cost $70. Ingredients: salt. That's it,' it says." she stopped herself here to try to stop laughing. Then she continued.

"'Where to buy: Walmart.'" Veronica stopped to wipe her eyes with her handkerchief. "'Instructions,'" she continued to read. "'You get a thingy from the house and you put it in the hot thingy. Turn on the hot thing and it can burn so you have to be careful. You make like something and put it in and it cooks. Then you get a plate and finish it.'" Veronica could hardly finish she was laughing so hard. Finally, taking a deep breath, she concluded. "And then he says, 'Don't leave the plate on the table; you have to throw it away in the sink or the flies will get on it.'"

Again, the whole van was laughing. "Whatever next?" Ruthie asked and then commented, "Out of the mouths of babes, *eh?*"

Then Hazel spoke again. "I made the best-ever Haystack meal the other night."

"What do you put in yours?" Franny wanted to know.

"Well, first I take the Saltines and put them in a brown bag and crush them with a rolling pin running over 'em. Then I do the taco chips or Nacho Doritos like that, too. I let 'em build their own haystacks, so I fill the buffet. Next, I shred the lettuce pretty fine and mince a bowl of hard-boiled eggs, each in their own bowl. Then there's a bowl of salsa—I canned a bunch last summer, then chopped up onions, green peppers, tomatoes, each in their own bowl, again. Then I cook the baked beans and crumbled sausage together. I put it on the stove early in the morning. I serve that hot. Let me see, what else? A bowl of grated cheese and then, uh, um?" she said frowning, trying to jog her memory.

"Maybe avocado?" Mrs. Dyck suggested.

"If I can find any, yes, thank you," Hazel replied.

"Oh, chopped green onions if you want, and sour cream. Then *queso* cheese sauce served up hot too and the chipotle dressing, to top it off. I almost forgot: the hot rice, I usually put some wild rice in with the white rice; we like it that way. Crunchy," she concluded. "You *chust* let them make their own that way." They all oohed and aahed then, already practically tasting all those flavors mixed together.

Veronica finally composed herself and became serious. "Other than that, not a whole lot going on. Except if you call a suitor wanting to get to know you 'from afar' something."

No one laughed at that. No cat calls or whistles from the peanut gallery. This was so unexpected. Out of the blue. Truly as unexpected as a buggy accident. Suddenly there was dead silence in the van. No one spoke but all eyes were on Veronica as she explained.

"Some bishop in Canada knows someone down this way who told him about me and now I am getting all these letters and I know I should have ignored it all, but I can't get rid of him now. I am really not interested after everything I went through. I am *chust* grateful I am not in like Rest Haven or Oaklawn, *ya* know? I mean, really, I could have *chust* lost it all those years ago and not come back. Some do, *ya* know." They all nodded in agreement. She went on.

"So, he is looking for a *frau* and for the life of me I can't figure out why they can't find him a wife in all of Canada, for pity's sake." She blew her nose into her handkerchief.

"He's forty and has one *kinner*. And—get this—he was a schoolteacher up there. An *Amishsche* MAN schoolteacher. He's farming with his *bruder* these days. I am thinking I'll *chust* not answer now at all. It'll die a natural death, is my way of thinking. My last letter that I wrote was supposed to completely turn him off, but it did *chust* the opposite! He's pig-headed if you ask me," she said shaking her head. "Positively bullish."

"You sure you don't want to even meet him?" Hazel wanted to know.

"Well, I think I'd meet him but be clear if you're sure you aren't a match," Ruthie said.

"Maybe he *chust* needs to find out for himself that you are decided," Matilda added.

"But..." Hazel ventured. "I wouldn't decide so quickly. I'd seriously pray about it and share it with your *grossmammi* or minister's *frau* or someone. You can't say if *Gott* has a plan here maybe, *eh?*"

"I *chust* don't know," Veronica moaned. "Maybe, but I haven't stopped praying since the first letter came. I am *chust* not interested. I always said I wouldn't marry again. I don't need a *halsband.* And I don't want one. I would always be a nervous wreck every time he took the buggy out. It took me a whole year almost *chust* to get myself back on a buggy bench. I'd *chust* be waiting the whole time for another *halsband* to up and die on me. No thanks. No way," she said, frowning and shaking her head. Another honk into her handkerchief.

Mrs. Dyck surprised them all then. "Well, honey. I've gotta tell *ya,* I am on my second hubby now. He's a real sweetie, too. We've been married ten years already. My first husband had a massive heart attack at fifty. No warning. Right after dessert one night. At the table. Left me with two teenagers. We got by and them two went off to college. Then I met my Dennis at church. Love at first sight. It's been worth it. They don't die until it's their time, honey. You can't worry about that. God will worry about that. You don't have to...." And then as an afterthought she added, "I think I had sliced black olives on my haystack last time, too."

Veronica hesitated and then spoke again. "And if I got pregnant again? I know I couldn't bear losing another *bobbel.* No one should have to go through that. What if all my *kinner* are born with it? Maybe it's hereditary. Who knows? No. No way. Not me," she vigorously shook her head again. "Even if we were allowed to use contraception, which we aren't, *ya* know, I'd still worry all the time. I'd go completely *fa-rechth*. I wouldn't sleep—you remember how long it took me to pull out of it last time, even having to take all those pills for the depression? It was hell. Literally. Once was enough. Too much if I'm honest. No one should have to bury a child and then a husband a year later. No one. I couldn't bear it," she said as her voice died down to just a whisper. Out came the handkerchief once more as hands reached out to touch or pat and reassure Veronica that they had heard her, and it was going to be okay. Somehow, it would all be okay.

CHAPTER 7

Bitty Lambs

Although she was thoroughly spent after her day out with the girls Veronica decided to write for a while before bed. It had definitely been a *gut* day. And that lunch at Perkins! She still thought they could do better on some of their pies, though. A bit too sweet in her opinion, but who'd asked her? Before she could change her mind, she opened her box of good stationary to begin a letter to Henry. It had been over a week that she'd been ignoring him, no, not really ignoring him, just *trying very hard* to ignore him. Her level best.

Dear Henry,

Greetings in our dear Lord's Name!

The garden is definitely kumming *along. I'll be canning here before too long. That is always fun, though I don't know if I'd enjoy it so much if I had a dozen* kinner *to feed all winter. Even with the nine of us in our family growing up the canning could turn the whole house into a veritable factory. Meals would get simplified down to cold sandwiches or canned soup and crackers more often than not,* chust *so all the work could get done for that day and we wouldn't have to stay up late cleaning it all up. No,* Mamm *made sure the canning and cooking would stop by dusk and then the cleanup would be all done in time for a late supper. Simple that would have to be, too. Soup and crackers again or maybe cheese slices and such, most likely.* Brode, *peanut butter spread, ya know.*

I was a schoolteacher for four years before I married. I loved teaching. Each year I'd have up to twenty of my very own kinner *all day long. Smart ones, simple ones, rebellious* kinner--*I adored them all. I loved being able to continue learning right along with them. I went to the little local library in town almost every week-end. At first the books I read were* chust *chosen at random. Then I discovered another one here, or another one there. Other Amish schoolteachers would get together during the year and share lists of their favorite books for the teachers and another list to read to the children and other aids they had discovered. Then I started picking up books at the thrift stores, too. One book would mention another book which would then mention another and so on. I had to read that one, too. I could never get enough. I eventually ended up reading philosophy and sociology, history, and the classics. I wished I could continue my education.*

For years I fanaticized that I wasn't born Amische *and could actually go to college, but then, in the end, I decided I liked being* Amische *too much and could never leave, but I could educate myself. I'd never have to stop reading. I realized that I didn't need a framed diploma hanging up somewhere telling me what I'd studied. I guess I've read more than most* Amische *fraus, but then there are some men, too, who devour books like I do. It isn't forbidden outright, but it is inferred in the Church that too much learning can be a temptation and affect one's life of simplicity; that worldly knowledge doesn't hasten one's journey to Heaven and might even curtail it. The thing is, it has never made me want to leave and go all* Englische. *I don't feel that I am any better or smarter than anyone else here.* Chust *perhaps a tad nerdy or eccentric, which folks kind of ignore I think, if they even notice at all. Which I doubt they do. Notice. I don't spout off all sorts of knowledge or get into theological discussions either like some* bruders. *No, I* chust *think a lot and talk to the Lord about it all, and marvel at His world and all it contains.*

Sorry I got off rambling there. My mind never stops. Sometimes I wish I was born simple. I really do. Life would be so much easier without all these ferhoodled *thoughts,* ya *know? But* Gott *decided otherwise.*

I was the fourth of seven children. We were a happy lot. Mamm *made sure of that.* Dat, *too. Most of the time one or the other of them was always surprising us and making us laugh.* Dat *would come in from the barn at the end of the day and give us the latest statistics on the new lambs: two boys and five girls*—chust *like us, two sets of twins and three singletons. All alive. All thriving. No rejects we'd have to bottle feed and keep by the wood stove in the kitchen. I loved caring for the rejected baby lambs though. That was my best thing ever. That happened more often when there were triplets and the ewe thought two was quite enough, thank you very much, and wouldn't feed the third. Or a bitty runt that she'd figure wasn't worth the effort. Then he would baa*—Dat would— *and we'd start laughing and couldn't stop. And he wouldn't stop, even as he came to the supper table.* Mamm *would swat him on the head with a potholder but that didn't stop him, either.*

Well, I should end this and get to sleep. I had a wunderbar *day out shopping with some of my single* frau *buddies, but now I am exhausted. Sending prayers for you and little Rose.*

Friend Veronica

She stuffed the letter into an envelope and stuck a stamp on it with a the briefest of prayers: *Not my will but Thine be done, Father.*

CHAPTER 8
Plastic Daisies

The knocking at the back door woke Veronica from a fitful sleep. There it was again. She leapt out of bed and ran to the bedroom window. Looking down from there she recognized her aunt's buggy. No one else in the district—most likely in the entire *Amische leute* had a bunch of plastic daisies wired onto the front window frame near the roof of the buggy. Her Aunt Pennelope was the only person she knew that sported a bunch of aging plastic flowers on her buggy. The way Pennelope explained it was that after church Sundays she didn't have time to walk up and down the rows of dozens of buggies parked in some field looking for her own. Sure, she should know hers, with the strips of duct tape holding the driver's door hinge on, but then she'd still have to walk around each buggy to get a closer look. Finally, she tied the daisies on which made it so much easier on Sundays, or when she went to *frolics,* or to one of the Amish stores in one of the nearby towns. For sure it wouldn't be sanctioned by the local bishop, but no one would begrudge an older sister for such a little thing. But then, some *Amische* districts were actually dividing their entire congregations over the whole issue surrounding the state-mandated orange triangular 'slow moving' signs. Some called it a worldly decoration. Others said it was simply for safety.

Aunt Pennelope wouldn't care if Veronica came downstairs in her nightie and robe. A quick check in the mirror to make sure she wasn't a complete fright before running down the stairs. Before she came into the kitchen, Pennelope had let herself in—most Amish didn't feel the need to lock their doors—and was hanging her shawl on a peg by the wood stove.

"What is so important that you've *kumm* at this hour?" Veronica queried, blinking herself awake.

"Oh, I *chust* wanted to check that my favorite niece wasn't lonely out here all by herself," her aunt answered.

"I'm *gut*. Really. Pretty used to it now, I guess. It's only been seven years on my own, don't *ya* know. But then, I do keep busy, *ya* know." Veronica finished buttoning her robe as she headed toward the wood stove to stoke up the coals left there from the night before. Pennelope grabbed the coffee pot from the stovetop and rinsed it out at the kitchen sink before filling it with fresh water from the gravity tank housed upstairs that fed the downstairs water tap.

"So, you're keeping busy?" her aunt continued as Veronica stoked up the fire in the stove.

"Between the garden, the yard, the sheep and chickens, my writing, and my single ladies' group, the *frolics* and our little adventures, *ya*, I am plenty busy. No time to brood," Veronica explained, assuring her dear aunt there was nothing to be alarmed about.

Then Pennelope laughed. "I *chust* remembered that first year after you lost your Amos. How keen certain *fraus* had been to get you hitched up again. Professional matchmakers, they imagined themselves."

Veronica shook her head in agreement. "I know. Pretty crazy. *Fa-rechth* for sure," she chuckled, "and they're still at it, too," she grumbled.

"Really? It hasn't died down? You aren't joshing? Remember that first one?" Pennelope asked.

"You mean Evan? *Ya.* Sending his buddy to ask me out on a date like we were still *youngie.* I sent him back packing pretty quick. Twenty years older than me, wasn't he? No wonder he was a bachelor. I don't think he knew what a bathtub was for either. Ugh!" Veronica shivered just thinking about it, sending Pennelope into the giggles.

"Well, but then, maybe a *frau* would *redd* him up a bit. You never know..." Pennelope said.

Then Veronica added, "Remember the widower with thirteen *kinner?* She died during childbirth with the last one. They waited too long to call for any help. That one was out in Tennessee. So unnecessary. So sad. Maybe pride or didn't think they needed any *Englischers* around there."

"I know," Pennelope agreed frowning and shaking her head.

Veronica set the coffee pot on a quilted hot pad on the table then. Opening her icebox, she took out the little Mason jar of camel milk, setting it by the mugs she'd put out earlier. The icebox was a little solid maple constructed thing, lined with galvanized steel. A block of ice that had been harvested last winter rested on a corrugated metal shelf which allowed for the ice to melt with the water passing through a tube in the bottom of the compartment to a flat pan located under the icebox to catch the water. Some finer models have spigots for draining ice water from a catch pan or holding tank. After the men in the district cut the ice blocks from the nearby lake during the coldest winter days, it is stored in a barn. The layers of blocks are carefully covered in saw dust and that way, would not melt for quite a while. The blocks are delivered or picked up from the barn. Horse-drawn flatbeds are used to haul the fresh-cut ice from the lake to the storage barn.

"I have some Hobo *brode* and jam I was going to have for breakfast. You'll have some, won't you?" Veronica asked, hopeful her dear aunt would stay and visit.

"*Ya,* for sure," her aunt said, settling herself at the table.

"Then it must have been a few months later I got that letter from somewhere in Pennsylvania. I forget where. Saloma wrote telling me about a widower there that she was so sure would make such a great match for me."

"Remind me which Saloma that was," Pennelope asked.

"Oh, *ya* know. My cousin Omar's *frau,*" Veronica explained as she pushed the little jar of sweet Amish peanut butter spread closer to Pennelope.

"What kind of *Amische* name is Omar?" Pennelope laughed. "Ooooh, I love this stuff. *Denki,*" she added as she scooped out a generous spoonful, plopping the sweet treat onto her bread. "Do you add any corn syrup or brown sugar to this along with the marshmallow fluff? Some make it that way. I think it's fine without it, *chust* the marshmallow alone."

"No. I make it with *chust* the fluff and peanut butter in equal parts. But back to Saloma, she said it means 'eloquent' and 'magnificently handsome.' Kind of funny, *eh?* I don't think I could name a *bobbel* 'Omar' myself."

"I know," Pennelope agreed, with a tiny shake of her head while sipping her coffee.

"Well anyway, Omar's friend Asher—I don't know what it was about that family that chose such *ferhoodled* names— he was like eleven years *younger* than me. Barely old enough

49

to marry, really. He didn't deserve to be stuck with me. I guess a bit of a renegade that they wanted to fix up quick with a wife before he got into any real trouble. As if that would stop him. Cute, they said. But that wouldn't make up for his unfaithfulness, though, *eh?* No way," Veronica said, her furrowed brow expressing the fact that she was still feeling concerned by that prospective match.

"Yikes. I'd forgotten about that one. You sure do get some wild ones, *eh?*" Pennelope wondered aloud, shaking her head and laughing.

"And Saloma wrote again a while later telling me all about that saddle maker down south somewhere. Do you remember him? What was his name?" Veronica asked, frowning. "He'd lost his wife to cancer recently."

"Was that... Thomas?" Pennelope wondered aloud. "*Ya,* I remember him."

"We actually met a couple of times," Veronica said. "He was young, nice enough, but I kept thinking he had no commitment to our way of life. *Chust* sort of putting in his time, *ya* know? Not excited about anything. Life was *chust* a drudge. You do what is required, no more, no less, and then you're done, *ya* know? It took me a while to figure out what it was about him. I knew I wanted someone excited about our life. Happy to be *Amische.* Seeking Jesus. I *chust* didn't get any of that from him. My parents were still living then, and they thought he could change with the right person, but I'd seen enough to know you have to take what you get, as he is now, not what you think you can mold him into. He had two little *buwe,* besides. I kind of felt sorry for those little boys. Sure, he would work and take care of his family, but he had no joy in it, or for those *kinner,* for that matter either. Didn't pay any attention to them. Didn't seem to play with them, either, or josh them around like some *dats.* It baffles me that he'd even want a wife, but then he'd have someone to cook and clean and sew and all that, I figure. Pretty dismal picture, if you ask me."

"No, I think you're right about that," Pennelope agreed.

"But I can't see a marriage of convenience, living parallel lives under the same roof, him *chust* dragging about and the *mamm* trying her darnedest to make it a happy home," Veronica insisted. "No, I think both should be pulling together, each one hundred percent. Or more. Otherwise, what message does that give your *kinner?* Will they grow up to be *gut dats* without a *gut* role model, and only the example of a hands-off one?"

"I don't stop praying for you, though, that *Gott* would find you the perfect *halsband* to grow old with, to be a companion," Pennelope assured her.

"But I am not lonely, my dear auntie," she went on. "I keep busy, and I am not fretting about accidents or babies *kumming* too early anymore, thank the Lord." Veronica continued to explain, "But I am still not about to get married again. And I know I couldn't risk having *kinner,* not after last time." She hesitated and then added, "...um, maybe we could talk about something a bit happier, Aunt Penne-lope?" Veronica requested then.

"Sure," Pennelope quickly agreed, while buttering another piece of bread. Then as an afterthought, "*Ya* know, my cousin I told you about? Moriah? Well, she *chust* got married. She's out in Ohio. Berlin, maybe. She's thirty-nine, too. Never married. Smart as all get out. And she paints. Beautiful scenery, especially. Something of an odd duck. Unique. Totally original. My *mamm* said, 'Gott broke the mold after that one.' And she doesn't care what anybody else thinks. *Chust* doing all these things you wouldn't expect. Painting, woodworking.

One year she shingled their whole outhouse. She cut the cedar shakes out and *chust* started nailing them in place and kept going till it was all done. Wants to know how everything works, *ya* know? I don't think she was ever even interested in marrying. She kept the house after her *mamm* died. That must have been a *gut* decade ago now. She milked the cows, helped with butchering, you name it. She ran the cider press whenever we had a *frolic* for the apples in the fall. She'd built some kind of cart to hitch onto the back of her buggy and carted the press around wherever they wanted it. A few days here, then a few days there. Anyway, she was a real *gut* worker, and always so cheerful. Quirky sense of humor, I tell *ya*."

Pennelope continued. "So, a family moved in near me. Must have been back about three years ago now. Their bachelor son still lived at home, helping his aging parents keep the farm up. He was for sure the quiet one. Not morose or anything. Great big fellow. Strong, taming horses to sell, *chust* working hard and driving his folks around all the time to visit or go to town or to the doctor. He was really *gut* to them.

"So, Moriah came to visit me one time and decided to check my fences while she was at my place. Always looking out for me. Well, this one time she was walking fences, and came in and started asking me about the new neighbors. I didn't know too much. I told her what I knew. Then I didn't see her for a spell. Next thing I know she tells me she wrote to the bishop and told him she wanted to get to know the fellow. Whatever next, right? Who does that? I'd never heard of such a thing. A woman asking about a *bruder*. Well, so the bishop talked to him one Sunday and suggested they get to know each other. The chap told the bishop he wasn't at all interested in dating. How could you even tell if she was the right one anyway, he says. He wasn't interested but because of the bishop, finally agreed to meet her. They wrote back and forth for a while, getting to know each other 'from afar' as they say. I sure don't know what all was in those letters but then she *kumms* to visit me and tells me they are courtin'. I couldn't have been more *erschtaunlich*. So, then they set the date and here she's married. Wonders never cease, eh?" she concluded. "You *chust* never know, do *ya?*" she said as she reached for the breadbasket.

"Did I ever tell you what Amos' *mamm* told me once?" Veronica began. "She caught me fixing the pencil sharpener on the sideboard over there with a screwdriver. It had *kumm* loose. She got this horrified look on her face and told me in no uncertain terms that I should never ever do that again, that I was taking away work from my *halsband,* and rather, actually demeaning him by doing it myself, as if I should ask him to fix everything and make believe I didn't know anything about anything besides being a *frau*. That I was attacking his masculinity, even."

Penelope nodded. "Yup. I heard that too once. That generation had some strange thinking, *ya* know." They pondered this while slowly sipping another mug of coffee each.

"But I haven't told you about my recent letters, have I?" Veronica asked.

"No. What letters?" Pennelope wanted to know, while reaching for the dish of apple butter. She looked up then to see Veronica's raised eyebrows just peeking over the rim of her coffee mug as she sipped the creamy coffee, which let Pennelope know there was another story *kumming*. This wasn't the end of it. Far from it.

CHAPTER 9
Camel Milk

The next morning as she dished up her breakfast of baked oatmeal there came a rap on the kitchen door. She turned from the wood stove and saw her cousin coming through the mud room.

"Why, Ruth Lapp! What brings you all this way? *Kumm* in. Have you eaten yet? I've got plenty here," Veronica offered.

"No, I've eaten. But I'll have a *kaffi* with you if you have enough," she said.

"*Mitt milch?*" Veronica asked.

"*Ya, denki,*" Ruth answered. Veronica grabbed a large mug from the hutch cupboard in the kitchen and filled it with coffee from the pot on the stove. She added the milk then and handed it to her friend.

"Mmmmm," Ruth purred. "It's really *gut, ya?*"

"Uh huh," Veronica agreed, smiling. Then slyly added, "It's camel milk."

Ruth plunked down the mug hard on the table. "What?" she demanded, her lips curled in apparent disgust.

"I am lactose intolerant, don't *ya* know, and the co-op in

town is now selling camel milk from an *Amische* farm called Humpback Dairies in Miller, Missouri. It's better, I think, than goat milk," Veronica explained. "I *chust* missed milk so much in my cereal and my *kaffi* and then I discovered this."

"How do you even milk a camel, do *ya* think?" Ruth wondered aloud, glaring down into the offending drink.

"Well, I read that they have to have the baby camel in the same pen, otherwise the *mamm* won't let her milk down. They give up to three gallons a day. Interesting, isn't it?" Veronica asked.

Ruth gingerly took another sip. "Can you cook with it too then?" she wanted to know.

"Yes, though I don't bake for myself so much. If I am bringing something for a potluck, I might pick up some regular milk for that. Otherwise, this is all I use now," Veronica said.

Ruth slowly sipped another mouthful. "I guess I could get used to it if I had to," she wagered cautiously.

"Now tell me why you've *kumm*," Veronica asked sitting down at the table.

"Well," Ruth began. "You know I've been apprenticing with that birthing clinic in Shipshewana for a year now. They have five licensed midwives and they let me shadow them on clinic days and then at births. I have learned so much and I even passed my state certified professional midwifery test. I can only practice now with doctor backup and the clinic doctor has approved me, too. Well, the problem is there are so many *Amische mamms* due this coming month that I need to have a plan so everyone ideally gets two midwives when they are ready. Most are home births but not all. Hudson, Wisconsin's hospital is still one of our favorite places when the *mamms* have any complications or can't have a home birth for whatever reasons, higher risk issues, *ya* know. So, the clinic makes up this rota and tells us when we are on and can be paged during those days or nights. You *chust* never know," Ruth stopped for another gulp of coffee, after carefully sniffing it first. It was slowly growing on her, the idea of camel milk, that is.

"More yet?" Veronica asked.

"Sure, *denki,*" Ruth answered, holding out the mug as she continued. "So, *ya* see, I need someone on this end for *chust* in case I get two overlapping *bobbeli kumming*. I can't leave anyone high and dry, so to speak. So, I have a pager, and I will get a call from one of the other midwives but if they get too booked up, I want to have an assistant with me at the very least. I don't want to go totally solo yet. And I'm wondering if I could have you on call? My driver would pick me up first and then you, and I'd *chust* have that assurance that I'd have a helper if they can't spare one to *kumm* from the clinic."

Veronica was floored. "I wouldn't know the first thing about it!" she protested.

"But see, you wouldn't need to. I'll fill you in on a few things first, and then you would *chust* follow my lead. We can only do the lowest risk births at home. When a baby is born at home, and the *mamm* has been cleared for a home delivery, things most often go really well, and you practically don't have to do anything at all. If that changes during the labor, we are trained to look for problems and can transfer them to the hospital then *before* we are in really hot water. We don't wait for things to get worse. Even if their blood pressure is up only one degree above what our protocols list, we are required to transport them, and the doctor will be there to meet us on the other end. He might agree to let us assist him then, or even let us deliver if he can get things back on track." Ruth waited a minute to let that all sink in.

Veronica just shook her head in disbelief. Finally, she was able to speak. "I for sure didn't see that *kumming*. Me, a midwife. I don't even know what normal is supposed to look like. *Mamm* never wanted us around when her time came. We'd get shuttled off to *Grossmammi's* or something. Are *ya* sure there isn't anyone else you can call who'd make a better helper?"

"No, because I can't ask a *mamm* who has her hands full already and can't *chust* drop everything at a moment's notice. Don't *ya* see? You'd be perfect," Ruth said trying to sound encouraging.

Veronica was unconvinced. "What'd you do if I fainted or something?" Veronica wanted to know, still visibly shaken.

"Oh, you won't. Don't you worry about that," Ruth assured her. "It is the most amazing thing in the whole world. Time stops. You never get tired of it. It is a miracle that you get to witness each and every time. You start praying the moment you get that call and don't stop until they're safely here. Then you start to look forward to the next one. You have a clean set of clothes ready every day, and your bag packed and by the door. It is quite exciting when you are gonna be the first person to meet that baby, the very first person in the entire universe, besides the Lord. You'll see."

"Are you sure? You are *really* sure there's no one better you could ask?" Veronica's voice squeaked with panic.

"Look," Ruth began. "I can't ask a *mamm* with a bunch of *kinner* to be on call twenty-four hours a day. I can't ask some single *youngie* who isn't really mature enough to be discreet and willing to learn. I am running out of options here. You'd be perfect. Really." The room was quiet then, save for the flapping curtains at the window. Veronica got up to tie back the blue curtains, still mulling over Ruth's very unexpected invitation. *That was for sure out of the blue,* Veronica thought to herself. *Even more of a shock than a buggy accident....*

"Oh, and I wanted to tell you about the quilting bee

we're having on Wednesday. Over at Orla Matilda Lapp's place. Their Marvin is getting married in the fall. Matilda did the quilt top and it's on the frame and ready. I saw it, too, a real masterpiece. That appliqued tulip pattern. Not easy. Definitely not for novice quilters."

"When is that?" Veronica asked.

"Next Wednesday. All day. Potluck," Ruth replied.

"I haven't been to one since last year," Veronica remembered. "Let's hope it's *gut* driving weather. At least they aren't waiting till the middle of winter for this one." Ruth nodded her agreement with that.

CHAPTER 10
Dear Kitty

Dear Kitty,

I am calling you Kitty after Anne Frank's diaries. She named them Kitty, too. Precious girl. I think of her often. How could people be so cruel, really? I will never understand that. Never. The Holocaust was so horrid. So very evil. Ach!

Veronica got up from the breakfast table to refill her coffee mug from the blue enamel pot on the wood stove. Carrying her empty cereal bowl to the sink she returned to the table and sat down once more and gazed out the window. It was a beautiful balmy day. The sun was just coming up over the corn field to the east. There were the last of the crocuses ringing the house. The daffodils would all be gone soon and need braiding. That kept the garden somewhat tidy when it was time to put the gardens to bed for the winter. But there were birds everywhere. She'd filled the bird feeders by the windows in the kitchen and had been handsomely rewarded with flocks of goldfinches, their feathers just beginning to turn from a gray-yellow to brilliant hues, at least the males' feathers would. Just this morning she saw her first ever rose-breasted Grosbeak. She even had to pull out her old copy of *Birds of America* to find out what it actually was.

Yesterday, while she was filling the feeders a red-winged blackbird had attacked her. To be more specific, it attacked her braid. She didn't see it coming but felt something flapping on the back of her head and tried slapping it away, thinking it might be a bat. It flew up to the gutter on the roof above the door and scolded her from up there. "Well, hello to you, too. You are friendly or what?" she asked it. When she turned back to the feeders it attacked again. *It must be making a nest,* she thought to herself, *and she thinks my hairs will make a nice, soft one for her babies. Whatever next?* she thought as she hurried back indoors while still trying to cover the long braid with both her hands.

The cardinals were still around too, as were the starlings and the purple martins. She'd read the book *Arnie the Darling Starling* to her classes each year when she taught school and ever since then hoped she'd find an abandoned baby starling to raise herself. Wouldn't that be *wunderbar-gut?* Then she remembered the baby crow her brother had snatched from a nest when he was only twelve. He'd climbed the tree and just lifted out one of the fat squawking babies. It looked like a plucked chicken. Only the first feathers had sprouted but could that thing set up a racket when it was hungry. Her brother would soak dog food in warm water and fed it with a long tweezer, stuffing the bird's crop full, the same way a parent would, one tidbit at a time. She couldn't remember what he'd named it, but she remembered how it would fly off his arm when he took it outside and always come back to him. Like it thought he was its parent.

Back then she started feeding it one day as it sat on the picnic table outside their back door squawking for its breakfast. It was getting bigger but apparently wasn't making any effort to forage for food on its own. In the meantime, her brother had stolen a baby owl from its nest in his next quest to study the species. She had worried that the crow wouldn't get enough to eat with her brother's new obsession with the owl, so she had started feeding it. All of a sudden, the crow started following her, as in everywhere.

They weren't allowed to bring the birds into the house. Their father built separate cages to put them in at night, but so far neither one strayed very far during the day, even though the hope was that they would return to the wild on their own one day. Rufus was trying to teach the owl how to attack prey by catching a live mouse himself and tossing it into the cage first thing in the morning. The owl wasn't interested in a roommate and ignored the rodent. Their father insisted that they stop providing any meals at all to the two birds and was sure they would find food pretty fast on their own then, which they did.

But the crow continued to think he was part of the family and would plunk himself down on the picnic table while they were trying to enjoy a summer supper out there. He would show up in the sand box at random, terrorizing the littlest children playing there. Finally, their dad insisted on bringing the crow to church one Sunday, leaving him in his cage in the buggy during the service and letting him loose just before they headed home. His raucous cries could be heard all the way from the buggy to the service inside. Several heads had turned when they'd heard it, which sent Veronica and her siblings into gales of giggles, though they were forced to cover their mouths with both hands to stifle themselves should they be heard and later disciplined for such inappropriate church behavior. It was a good forty-five-minute drive home in the buggy, but that bird still found his way back to them, showing up for breakfast right on time the next day.

In the end, their dad handed the cage over to a van driver who was picking up folks in the area with strict instructions not to let it out until they were as far away as possible from the settlement. They never did see that crow again. Their mother consoled them by saying it was time he go out and find himself a wife and that he might even fly back with her someday just to visit, to introduce her to us, she said. Then she remembered: Rufus called him Poe. As in Edgar Allan, even if he wasn't exactly a raven. Most likely a common crow.

She shook her head then, thinking back to Ruth Lapp's request the night before. Absurd. Her, an assistant midwife? It was the last thing she'd ever dreamed of doing. Did she want to? Would she even be a help or only get in the way? Putting the idea out of her head once more she picked up her pencil to continue writing.

> *So what do you think, Kitty? It's absolutely* ferhoodled, *eh? I agree. Ruth said she'd drop by today and give me a pager from the clinic so she can let me know when she needs me. I guess I can try one birth and she'll realize I am not at all suited to the work. She'll see pretty quick, I wager. I did lay out a clean dress and* kapp *and packed a purse. I put in a clean apron and some snacks. How do you even know how soon to go? Or when the* bobbel *might be born?*
>
> *Well, it's pretty crazy if you ask me. Back to my book, I guess, not that I'll ever get published. I read that Laura Ingalls Wilder didn't even begin to write her books until she was in her forties, forty-four exactly, and wrote until she turned ninety! So maybe there's still hope for me.*

She flipped through the pages she had written the last

time she'd opened the composition book and read the last entry there. Picking up where she'd left off, she continued writing.

That kitchen was especially big for an Amish farmhouse. Dat had built onto the original house after Rufus was born. He was number three. The first, twins, came before him. That's Tamar and Avram. I came next after Rufus. Then another set of twins, Zaidi and Zophie. Zorah is the baby. I think Mamm was happiest when she was either in the family way, or caring for all of us, though the two overlapped quite a bit. I figured out once that Mamm was expecting or nursing a baby (or both at the same time) for a total of nine consecutive years. No breaks in there, and it made her happy. Dat too. He often said while gazing at all of us around the supper table with that silly grin of his on his face that his 'quiver was full indeed.' I didn't know what he meant till I was older and discovered Psalm 127. We all felt wanted and loved, even when he had to teach us a lesson.

I remember Mamm telling us that one time after I was born, chust over a year after Rufus, she'd worried that he would get jealous having been the baby all that time. She thought to kind of prepare him and when he first saw me, she told him I was his 'very own sister' and now he was a big brother, a very important job, for sure. She was really afraid he'd resent me for displacing his idyllic position as the baby of the family.

So, she was washing the diapers one day soon after that and he came running into the kesselhaus *all upset and loudly told her, "Mamm, Mamm, my very own baby is crying!" She ran out of the room to check on the* bobbel *and found I was only hungry, but he had taken it upon himself to be my protector! So much for being jealous. She hugged him then and told him what a* gut *big brother he was.*

Ach! I am rambling here, she admonished herself. She

scribbled a question mark in the margin and circled it several times. She would revisit that paragraph later.

So, we had this great big kitchen. Life circled around the wood stove there. The long table was set in the alcove in the new part only a few feet away from the stove. The stairs to the upper level where the bedrooms were wrapped around, behind the stovepipe. An iron filigree grate in the upstairs floor was situated right above the wood stove, in the ceiling, and brought up all the warmth along with the good smells. Only occasionally burnt smells and smoke wafted upwards when one of the little ones managed to drop a toy onto the stovetop from the holes in the wrought iron in the grate, simply for the joy of watching the little plastic farm animal almost magically transformed there into a pink or brown puddle of goo. Within minutes it would turn black, bubble, turn to ash and finally smoke. The smoke alarm would go off then and Dat *would invariably run from the barn and* Mamm *would instantly slide whoever had been snuggled up in her lap onto the floor where they'd land with a thud, while she'd jump up from her rocker and run toward the kitchen.*

She'd frantically wave the big aluminum pot lid in the air above her head toward the smoke detector while pulling over the stepstool, climb up on it, and pull out the battery. By the time she'd done that Dat *was in the kitchen examining the little pile of soot on the stovetop up close while frowning, as several little pairs of eyes were watching from above through the iron grate. Finally, he'd slowly look up to the ceiling above the stove. That gaze would paralyze the little herd of kids up there. Of course, they were all guilty and promised never to do it again, fully repentant, tears and all, though that resolve quickly melted the next time there was a blizzard or a rainy day and we'd be cooped up once more.*

You can only make so many button strings or work on puzzles you've already put together a dozen times before or playhouse or sardines for so many hours or practice your penmanship or read books until you chust *had to jump up and think up some new adventure. We'd often sneak out to the barn when* Mamm *wasn't looking and bring back a tiny kitten each to play with. Or we'd take all our sock puppets and create a whole puppet show to put on that night for* Mamm *and* Dat *who would dutifully pull up their chairs and sit there laughing through the whole thing, clapping furiously at the end.*

One year we even hung a huge sheet up across the middle of the great room and with a couple of barn lamps hanging from the beam above, put on a play that way, all the actors now silhouettes behind the curtain. The audience would be seated at the other end of the room to watch. Mamm *would even make popcorn or sweet Cracker Jacks in huge bowls and serve hot chocolate afterwards. Always with mini marshmallows, too.*

She finished off the last drops of lukewarm coffee in her mug and sat higher up to stretch. That was enough journaling for one day. She smiled to herself. So many *wunderbar* memories. *So what happened? What changed my life after that?* She was tired and sad remembering the past. It was bittersweet. Then the thought came to her. *Oh, but there's that quilting bee today. I almost forgot. Well, but you can't be lonely really when you have such* gut *friends and are surrounded by the* bruders *and* schvestas. *I don't know how the rest of the world can cope without that. I shouldn't complain. We've really got it* gut. Denki, *Jesus.*

CHAPTER 11
The Quilting Bee

Everyone was looking forward to the quilting bee. Sure, it was a hassle getting all your *kinner* washed and off to school with their lunch pails, and then getting the youngest *redded* up for the trip—babies, toddlers, and preschoolers who wouldn't be in school yet. Then making sure you've left the house in presentable order, turned down the damper on the wood stove, and packed a generous dinner for the hubby to take to work. You had to load up the baby's *kalvi* with enough diapers for the day, remembering to put a diaper pail in the buggy for the soiled diapers, adding Fruit Loops or Cheerios or graham crackers and any other snacks to the basket. There would be some older girls who had already graduated from the eighth grade who would be at the quilting bee, having been employed to keep the little ones happy for the day.

It took planning but it was well worth it for such a fun day out. These *mamms* had been mostly staying home, 'keepers of the home' they were called. It was a vocation, a divine calling to be a wife and a mother. But it came at a cost: days and weeks staying at home tending to the *bobbeli,* the endless laundry, the garden, keeping the house clean and tidy, making sure the floors weren't littered with all sorts of toys causing a fall hazard if you weren't looking where you were going, (the little plastic stegosaurus and ankylosaurus were the worst things to step on barefoot with all those spiny plates on their backs.) Seeing to all the meals, all the canning, baking enough bread for the week, all the sewing for everything your family would need, it was endless.

Most weren't well off enough to just order trousers and shirts or dresses ready-made. There were plenty of places you could buy them, but they didn't come cheap. Sure, you could buy frozen peas and other vegetables already cleaned and shelled, and save all that time, but it wasn't the same. And your mother-in-law could always tell the difference for certain. And then there were all the sleepless nights with a colicky baby, or one with a cold who couldn't nurse and breathe through his nose at the same time and would get mad and frustrated and start screaming. The worst was when you realized that you were so terribly exhausted because you had another little blessing on the way and the morning sickness was getting out of control because you couldn't rest all day but just had to keep forging ahead. No, it was not easy. No one ever promised it would be. But then all of a sudden, they will all be grown up and flying the nest and you will actually miss all those years of trying to keep up with it all.

When she arrived, Veronica drove her buggy into the field by the side of the Lapp's old farmhouse. It had been added onto over the years. First the *dawdy haus* had been erected to house the grandparents, giving them a smaller place but still close by should they need any extra help as they got older. The main farmhouse had eventually sprouted numerous additions, too, one being a bigger open summer kitchen in the back where the breeze would keep them cool while canning or butchering. A newer *kesselhaus* was added next with new cement slab flooring with a central drain which made washing so much easier. It also housed its own wood stove so the hot water could be heated right there and wouldn't have to be hauled over from the big kitchen anymore.

Veronica unhitched her horse and led her into the paddock by the barn. Two more buggies had come in behind her so she waited to see if she could help them unpack or unhitch their horses. Both *mamms* arrived with full loads: Tupperware dishes to add to the lunch, packed *kavlis,* fussy *bobbeli* ready to be freed from their confines in the back. Veronica hefted up the *kavli* and hanging it on her shoulder by its leather strap, reached for the first squirming baby who immediately howled his disapproval of this person he didn't recognize.

"Oh, dear," Veronica gently cooed. Turning the baby around so he could see his mother, she pointed out, "there she is. You're *chust* fine, little guy. No need for that...."

"Oh, he *chust* started doing that. Funny thing isn't it?" his *mamm* chuckled as she lifted out a chunky toddler and set her down on her bare feet on the grass. The child started jabbering something to which the *mamm* nodded and heartily agreed. "*Ya.* Is that so?" she asked.

Veronica laughed, "Do you understand what she said?" she asked incredulously.

"Most of the time, no. I *chust* agree and she's happy. Last week," the *mamm* laughed, "I told her '*ya, ya'* when she was going on and on in the kitchen, and she looked up and asked again, and I was busy so I *chust* humored her, and didn't she pick up her *bruder's* toy firetruck and tossed it into to my pot of spaghetti I had boiling on the stove! I guess I'd said she could."

"Then a while ago, she was sitting in her highchair," the *mamm* went on, "and I'd given her one of her cardboard books with all the animals while I was finishing up making dinner, and she got all excited bouncing up and down and pointing to the corner of the kitchen and babbling up a storm. So, I asked if she'd seen a mouse, maybe. She shook her head and kept pointing, so I took the book and pointed to a mouse picture and she shook her head no, so I turned some pages and pointed to the different animals and she kept saying no, until we got to one page and she got all excited slapping the picture and kept saying something and slapped the page again and pointed like she'd found it. She was convinced it had been an alligator!"

"Oh no!" Veronica laughed out loud. "I hope you write these things down. They're priceless!"

"I know I should, but there *chust* isn't the time...." the *mamm* said then, chuckling, with her arms full, her *kapp* askew, her shawl falling off one arm, turning toward the back door, tugging the toddler along, the child's nose in desperate need of a wipe. At the same time her sodden diaper was making a bee-line toward her ankles. That's when Veronica noticed that the *mamm* was in the 'family way.' *I chust don't know how they do it. It can't get much harder than that, day in and day out,* Veronica thought to herself. *Maybe I shouldn't complain. I have it so much simpler. I guess we always think the grass is greener on the other side of the fence. But then, I am not so sure.... Am I sad I won't have that, too?* she pondered. "*Sometimes, if I am honest,*" she thought. Still hanging onto the baby who was still facing out, she breathed in his baby smell while kissing the top of his head. *There is nothing in the world like it,* she thought to herself. *Your will be done, then,* she prayed with a heavy sigh while her eyes stung like they always did when she tried not to cry.

Everyone was in the house unloading all their *klimbim,* changing diapers and sorting out mothers' helpers for the *kinner* for the day.

One *frau* could be heard saying, "Now, you be sure to bring her to me when it's time to nurse. She should sleep till then, I am guessing." Another *mamm* instructing one of the girls said, "He's allergic to peanuts, so don't give him anything that isn't in the *kavli.* You get that?" And another handing over her toddler said, "Watch out for this one. She's at that biting stage. Don't leave her out of your sight for a minute!"

The sofa in the great room was piled high with coats, bonnets, sweaters and shawls. The mud room appeared to be overflowing with shoes and sneakers, left there in an effort to keep the house clean—if that were at all possible. The kitchen table and the sideboard were crowded with Tupperware and covered casseroles vying for space. There were platters of cookies and bars, bowls of popcorn, and Chex mix. A giant urn was simmering on the wood stove, keeping the coffee hot for the invasion. Paper plates, napkins, and Styrofoam cups were stacked in the dry sink.

"Ooooh! Who brought pretzels?" Ruth asked above the din.

"I did. They're so *gut,* too," Mildred answered. "My mother had them sent from that pretzel factory in Akron, Pennsylvania. Clarence Martin has been making them there since the 1980s. I couldn't make them this *abbeditlilch* myself, as if I had time. I brought mustard too."

Veronica continued to peruse the offerings on the

oilcloth-covered table. Every leaf had been added to extend the already large oak table. The kitchen had been added onto the large farmhouse years earlier to accommodate the ever-growing community. Every other Sunday church was held in a different home throughout the district. The lunch afterwards would be served outdoors, weather permitting, but in inclement weather and during the colder months, the house or barn hosted the lunch, necessitating the larger rooms. Some entrepreneurial families have had the idea in recent years to offer authentic Amish dinners to guests during the busy tourist season. The room is then set for a hundred visitors (*Englischers* mostly) and dates are booked with tour groups. It has proved to be a lucrative side enterprise. A very lucrative one indeed.

Today the offerings included hot dishes: Baked Macaroni, Sweet Potato Casserole topped with walnuts, Potluck Potatoes covered in buttery corn flakes, Baked Cream Corn, a baked Ohio Filling, and Zucchini Egg Bake. There were baskets of breads and rolls, plenty of Amish Peanut Butter Spread, and too many desserts to count. These women were milking their one day out for all it was worth.

The *kinner* all sorted, it was time to think about quilting. The quilt had been stretched and pinned to the wooden frame. Folding chairs had been arranged around the four sides, three to a side. Spools of white quilting thread sat on the quilt top next to pin cushions and dishes of thimbles. Small scissors were laid out as well.

The quilt was exquisite; not an easy pattern to execute. Tulips were first carefully appliqued onto white squares. Three tulips per square. The tulips themselves were a deep burgundy cotton calico, the leaves and stems a forest green. The center of the quilt was equally beautiful.

A larger center resembling a lone star dominated there, an assortment of different colored dark and medium green calicos forming the star. The center would be quilted with a pie pan-shaped circle, stitched to look like a flower.

It was easy enough to quilt around the leaves and flowers, but the center's stitched pattern would have to be carefully drawn with chalk, using a template, or more often than not, a tin pie pan itself with the petals cut out of a cardboard cereal box that could be traced around. The borders of the quilt were a combination of straight pink calico lattices and then, beyond that toward the outermost edges, little triangles sewn together making long side borders.

Twelve *frau* could work on the quilt at the same time seated around the edges, adding a couple more at the corners of the frame. These ladies were experts. Perfect tiny stitches were forming all around the beautiful masterpiece. They'd all learned as little girls, first making their own dolly quilts, being taught the art by their own mothers and grandmothers.

"When is the wedding?" one woman asked.

"November, of course," the mother of the bride answered.

"Will he keep farming with his *dat?*" another asked.

"No. The brothers are going to expand the *dat's* broom business. It's going really well," came the answer from the north side of the quilt.

"How is that going?" another voice inquired.

"Really *gut*. They say they are now getting orders from all over the country," the same *mamm* replied. "Melvin has really made a name for himself. That family is doing well, too."

"It's amazing, all the new start-ups. I mean, not everyone can find *gut* farmland, *ya* know, and they've thought up these *ferhoodled* schemes. But they work."

"I know. Like I *chust* read about those Mennonite guys making a go of that coffee company down in Costa Rica."

"And the harness and tac shops and roofing companies,

too. Even the blacksmiths. We need them, too. Emily, please pass the scissors," Hazel said.

"Did you see that write up about the Amish tiny homes somewhere in Kentucky? On wheels? Now that's inventive. I think they're called Cedar Holler something."

"And they're *Amische?*"

"*Ya.* Absolutely. It's been a real success. Who would have thought?"

Heads were shaking—or nodding--as the women were concentrating on their stitches.

"What time is lunch?" Kate asked.

"We *chust* sat down. You're hungry all ready?" came a voice from across the quilt.

"I didn't get much breakfast with getting them all *redded* up for sure," Kate replied. At that she got up and helped herself to coffee and a donut from the dessert counter. She stood away from the quilt to sip her coffee and devour the fresh donut before returning to her place at the quilt. At the same time one of the babysitters brought a baby to his *mamm.*

"I'm gonna take him into the bedroom. He'll be too distracted to nurse here. I'll be right back," Heather announced as she left, the baby perched on her hip.

"Did *ya* hear, Raymond's Rachel had *ztzvilling* yesterday?" Dorothy asked.

At that everyone sitting there stopped sewing, straightened and looked up.

"No! Really?" Veronica asked.

"Yes, really," Dorothy chuckled.

"And they're all okay?" Kate asked.

"*Ya. Chust* fine. They can *kumm* home by the weekend," Dorothy informed them.

"So, she didn't need a C-section then?" Hazel asked.

"No. *Gut* size, too. One of each. She named them Ruth and Isaac," Dorothy continued.

"My *halsband* said he was going to name our twins Hunky and Dory," another *mamm* laughed. "Or Tweedle Dum and Tweedle Dee."

"*Ach!* That's awful," someone else groaned.

"It's a lot of work but it does get better. They play together all the time and don't need you as much as a single baby does. People still ask me if they're identical. I *chust* agree with them and let them figure it out. A boy and a girl *can't* be identical," she explained. Some at the quilt wondered about that, but wasn't that a possibility? Could it be?

Soon afterwards Veronica stood at the stove and announced, "*Kaffi* break then?" She proceeded to fill the mugs sitting by the stove and passed around the half and half and the pumpkin spice liquid creamer. Heather returned and carefully placed her tightly swaddled sleeping baby in the oak cradle in the corner of the room. Then taking a mug of coffee from Veronica she said, "I better get some sewing in. I've barely made a dent in it."

By noon the babysitters were descending on the tables of food for their hungry little charges. The *mamms* helped them make up the paper plates and settled all of the toddlers on the floor in the great room. Then everyone else filled their plates and found places to sit away from the quilt, avoiding any unwanted stains at this stage.

"Where can I get this recipe?" someone asked from the great room.

"Which one?" someone else asked.

"The Sweet Potato something," she replied.

"Oh, I got that from that new *Amish Soups and Casseroles* cookbook," came the answer.

And then the same *frau* added, "The whole title is *Amish*

Soups and Casseroles: Traditional Comfort Food Favorites," she quoted. "There are some really *gut* ones in there."

Then from the buffet at the kitchen table Hazel addressed the room: "Who had time to make Fudge Melt-aways? They're my favorite!"

A hand shyly went up at the farthest corner of the quilt. It was Ruth. "I did, but then I made them yesterday while I was making them for mine. They sure like them, too."

"Well, you must have a *maud* helping you because I can't imagine having a spare minute to do all that. Maybe you can loan her to me," Dorothy pouted.

"No, *chust* big girls that all want to be bakers when they grow up," Ruth chuckled. "Now all I have to do is get them to do the clean up after they bake. What a disaster! The kitchen looks like a tornado swept through when they're all in there," she added.

"I taught mine to fill the basins with hot soapy water *before* they even start mixing it all up and do the dishes along the way. It keeps it all under control then that way," another *frau* explained.

Someone else pointed out, "look at all these desserts. We're getting spoiled, ladies. Look! there's an upside-down pineapple cake! And there's those new Aussie Bites. Veronica, those must be yours! They are out of this world."

"What's in them?" came another voice. This time it was Hazel.

Veronica answered. "There are some recipe cards over on the sideboard with the recipe written out. I knew some would want it."

The rest of the afternoon flew by. It was getting to that time that the *mamms* needed to start packing up.

"Does anyone know where Ezra's blue shoes went to?" his *mamm* called out to any and all there who could help look for them.

"I think someone mistook my *kavli*. Can y'all look for it?" another *frau* shouted above the hubbub. Toddlers were lying on their backs on the floor having their diapers changed and arms were being shoved into coat sleeves for the long trek home. It was still light out. They'd be home in time to make a simple supper before their men folk came in. It had been a *wunderbar-gut* day. The food, the fellowship and friends meant so very much to each one. They'd for sure get plenty of milage out of such a fun day out.

We really are so blessed, Veronica thought as she steered the horse down the long dirt road heading home. *Denki Gott,* she prayed. Then that little niggling thought popped into her mind once again, seemingly from nowhere: *Those bobbeli, those toddlers, I wouldn't mind all the work for that. You don't think only about yourself anymore when you're that busy. You've given yourself over completely then,* eh?

CHAPTER 12
A Pumpkin Named Rufus

Veronica spent the morning in the garden once more. She loved gardening. She'd brought an old tin can out with her this morning to collect the slugs in. When she was little her *mamm* would send her out to the garden every morning with a saltshaker from the table to sprinkle salt on the little beggars. They'd curl up and die then. She didn't feel sorry for them. She'd been taught they were pests. Just like the rats in the barn. *Dat* had her help him in the evenings after supper while he poured Coca-Cola into old aluminum pie pans in the barn for the rats to drink. Supposedly they can't burp and die when they drink the stuff. It made her wonder if she'd die if she drank it, too. She'd never seen it at the table at home, though every so often it'd be there at the communal lunch after church on a Sunday. It made her wonder.

The green pea vines were almost to the top of the lattices she'd tied up. Tiny pea pods hung all over the plants, almost ready to start picking. She planned to blanch them for three minutes, dunking them in cold water next, and then sealing them up in bags to put in the kerosene chest freezer in the mud room.

Little cucumbers were sprouting everywhere. She looked at them, remembering the trick her *Dat* had taught them. He would get an old, clear root beer bottle that he'd saved, one with a skinny top and carefully thread in the little cucumber still attached to the vine into the narrow opening until it was almost to the bottom of the bottle. He'd lay it down on its side then. It would continue to grow there until it filled the bottle. Then he would cut the vine and fill the bottle—what little space was left—with vinegar and cap it closed. It was forever an object of conversation after that. How did that thing get in there anyway? You for sure couldn't get it back out without smashing the glass.

He would also carefully carve their names onto the little pumpkins and watermelons, when they first appeared, cutting away only the outermost rind and not puncturing the fruit. As they grew, the fresh scars would heal over and harden and expand into big names, each child claiming his or her personal watermelon or pumpkin. Rufus especially looked forward to his own personal pumpkin each year.

One year, while he was reading to them about the early Native Peoples of North America, he remembered something *Doddy* had told him about how they gardened and he wanted to try it as an experiment. He planted corn seeds in March in little mounds of dirt, three or four kernels to a mound and waited for them to sprout. Then he planted squash seeds and pole beans or little plants from the greenhouse around the base of the corn, in a circle. The pole beans climbed the corn as they grew. The corn grew faster so it could support the vines. They trained the squash vines around the outer edge on the ground of the beans and wrapped any new runners back around the corn. Each mound then produced all those vegetables in abundance.

They read about Almanzo growing a prize-winning pumpkin by feeding it milk, in the *Little House* books, too. *Dat* never had much luck with that scheme, though he tried unsuccessfully several years in a row. Supposedly a wick was inserted into the pumpkin flesh and the other end of the wick lay in a bowl of milk. He never did win a prize for his milk-fed pumpkins, though, try as he might. The last year she was home he managed to grow a pumpkin that weighed four hundred pounds. Before it reached one hundred, he put it onto a pallet to continue to grow there so it could be moved to the tri-state fair to be weighed and displayed. A neighbor with a forklift would have to be hired to get it there. Still, someone else beat that weight and got the coveted blue ribbon, some fellow from Anoka, Minnesota.

Just then the mail truck swung into her driveway, jolting her out of her memories of gardening with *Dat.* Veronica dusted off her hands and slowly walked barefoot through the grass toward the mailbox. When he drove away, she took out the mail he'd deposited there. Joann Fabrics coupons, a VFW fundraising fish fry flyer, *The Budget,* a hand-addressed leaflet from Mt. Morris, New York, advertising Katie's Mercantile and her latest spring collection of dress fabrics on offer, and...a letter. Of course. Two weeks to the day from the last one. He sure was punctual. She had to give him that.

Dear Veronica,

Greetings of love in Our Dear Lord's Name!

Finally, we can set out the seedlings in the kitchen garden and seed the fields. We'll be up early doing chores so we can work out there till dusk. It's always a mad rush this time of year. Especially after the slow pace all winter, hunkering down for months until the snow is gone with so little to do in the house. Chust *barn chores every day. Sure, we order seeds come Christmas and carefully plant them in the greenhouse in January and February, making sure it doesn't freeze in there. One year we experimented with geo-thermal heating and laid pipes underground and moved the greenhouse over that. We ran the wood incinerator day and night on low in that thing to keep it above freezing but I guess it was still too much and all the spinach was cooked one morning in late October when we went in. We got the whole district to* kumm *over and lift up the greenhouse—it was actually a pole barn we'd built with windows. It took over fifty* bruders *to lift the thing and walk it over to the new plot we'd cleared. We finally got it right and have it working* chust *fine this year.*

Rosie is growing like a weed. She talks non-stop now, though I am never quite sure what she is telling me. My bruder *has a bunch of* kinner *so she is growing up with a house full of older* bruders *and* schveshtas. *She is such a ray of sunshine. I only wish her* mamm *was still here to see her. It is still hard to believe sometimes. Even after all this time. Time is supposed to heal that. That's what folks say, anyway. Perhaps I am* chust *cynical by nature. I don't know....*

I was so grateful for your letter. It is gut *to hear about you and the goings on down there and your family. Are your parents still living? Mine are gone. They left my* bruder *and me everything and no debts, so we are well set up* gut.

I don't want to rush this at all but wonder if you are ready to visit? Tell me if it's too soon, please. I could kumm *there for a couple of days or you could* kumm *here, meet my family and the community. I want to meet you but only when you are ready. Enough said about that.*

We've been thinking that having the greenhouse, ya know, we could start growing flowers too and sell them either at the roadside or to the florists in the area. No others are doing that to my knowledge. It would keep us busy in the winter then. We grew some mums last year, and they went like hotcakes, especially right before Thanksgiving. They're super hardy and lasted quite well. We have the space out there so we might as well expand that a bit.

So, I thought I'd tell you a bit about my family. It was chust *my* mamm, *my* dat, *my* bruder *and me. There was a baby girl who died before me. She came early and* chust *wasn't strong enough to make it. Then I came along, a whopping ten-pound wood chopper. My* doddy *and* grossmammi *were living in the* dawdi haus *next door by then. That was super fine 'cause us* buwe *could escape over there if we'd gotten into any mischief and they couldn't find us.* Mamm *was always on to the grandparents about not spoiling us, but they couldn't help it. They were* chust *so happy to see us growing up. I don't think she knew they had a secret stash of horehound candies and snuck those to us all the time.* Mamm *was always on about how many cavities we got and never figured out who was to blame. And one year I even showed my* bruder *a trick I'd* kumm *up with. You could run your toothbrush under the water for a minute and then hang it back up. Next you leave the top on the toothpaste and pound it up a bit so it looks like we've brushed. And presto! No need to brush anymore. I thought that was pretty clever, eh?*

Dat's *favorite thing was camping. He'd get one of the* bruders *to take care of the farm for a weekend here or there and take us up north or wherever he'd figured out on his maps. We even got down to the Boundary Waters Wilderness Area in Atikokan, Ontario. He built a covered wagon with a canvas top and a hitch for two horses. He'd pack a tent, too, for* gut *weather and a Coleman stove with a dropdown kitchen counter like a cowboy chuck wagon.* Mamm *fussed about not having all her pots and pans, but we could tell she liked it too, figuring out how to cook on it, even making us donuts, and biscuits and gravy, and buckwheat pancakes. We'd fish and hunt and even ran into a bear once while we were blackberry picking. That* mamm *bear had two cubs with her. That's when I saw my* dat *scared. Really scared. I'd never seen him like that before. Well, we got outta there fast and he told us not to tell* Mamm. *We didn't, at least not until I was in my teens. Milo told on us. Was she ever mad, then. Boy! Told us that if she had known that we'd never have gone camping again.* Dat chust *winked at me from across the room when she said that.*

They were much older than most when they met and got married. That's why there were only us three kinner. *They were always grateful for our family. It was so sad when they got old and sick. Within a year of each other they died. I wanted Rosie to know them, but they were gone by then. You never know what life has in store for you, do* ya? *Well, I can only pray to be a* gut dat *and make sure she looks back too, at the happy times. Well, that's enough for now. Take good care of yourself and keep us in your prayers.*

Your bruder *in Christ,*
Henry

CHAPTER 13

Wunderbar-gut Memories

V eronica came in finally, stomping the dirt off her bare feet on the jute rug in the mud room entry. It was dusk. Starlings had been circling overhead on their way to trees where they would sleep. Sparrows were heading *en masse* to barns in the area for the night. The garden was coming along. It was easy to pass the time out there. Rewarding too. The days could be long and boring without a family to care for. Hobbies and visiting could take up only so much of one's time. Quilting didn't go as well in the evenings, even with a Coleman directly overhead when you were sitting at a quilting frame. She preferred sewing during the day, situating the quilting frame by a window. She'd recently bought a battery-powered head lamp to try out and see if she could use it to do more in the evenings, sewing or writing. It for certain helped and you could see without straining your eyes the whole time. Rebecca had suggested it to Veronica after she'd bought one for herself.

After a hot bath Veronica returned to the kitchen and assembled a cold supper. She lit the mantle lamp above the table and stoked up the wood stove to make some chocolate mint tea, her favorite. She grew it in a patch below the eves of the house. It was super hardy. Came up on its own year after year. She'd trim the stems of the longest tendrils and hang them in the kitchen behind the wood stove until the leaves were dried and then drop them into a Mason jar she kept the tea leaves in. The nights had a chill to them still, so a little warmth rising up to her bedroom wouldn't hurt.

Sliced fresh Hobo bread sounded *gut*. She'd made several loaves a few days earlier. It froze well, too, so she could make it last without molding. Her little kerosene-powered freezer kept things longer than the icebox. She had been experimenting with the camel milk and had actually made yogurt and butter from it, two things she thought she could never eat again. Maybe cheese would be next. Non-dairy cheeses at the co-op were all so expensive. It was worth a try. Some apple sauce and carrots sticks with hummus completed the meal.

Sitting down at the table, she remembered the encounter with Clara yesterday after church Sunday lunch. She had been recalling one particular minister's sermon. So encouraging. So thoughtful. As if he were speaking directly to her heart.

With a dozen or more *fraus* in the kitchen during the massive clean-up, all chatting in low voices, it sure made for a cheerful atmosphere. Veronica thought to herself, *no, I'm not lonely. I'm blessed. I am blessed with all these dear* schveshtas. *I will always have* schveshtas *and the* bruder *surrounding me....*Denki, Gott.

As if on cue, Clara squeezed in next to Veronica at the sink.

"Well, it's *gut* seeing you getting out more," Clara praised her.

"Uh-huh," Veronica hesitantly agreed, wary of what was coming next. How utterly ridiculous and impertinent that statement was. She'd been out and about for seven years, for pity's sake if she was referring to the buggy accident. *She'll try anything to prove her point,* Veronica thought to herself.

"Well, I wanted to let you know, remember I told you about Steven Troyer, the one whose wife ran off on him and then died?" Clara hurried on. "Well, he would have been a real prize. But he's met someone, and it looks pretty serious," she stated. "I wish you'd have given him a chance. I worry about you, *ya* know. You should have listened to me."

Veronica tried to quickly, and hopefully, dispel that statement. "I am not lonely. I do not want to remarry." She did not care how terse she sounded. It was time to put this woman in her place. "I do not want more *kinner.* I am completely content right how I am now," she explained, hoping to sound firm without sounding harsh.

"I know, dear, but you aren't thinking straight, not after all you've been through. Sometimes others can see it clearer than you can. You have to give it a try. Trust people who love you...." Clara insisted.

"So, who have you got for me now?" Veronica surrendered to the pressure knowing she couldn't fight Clara. Stubborn Clara. Had she always been this pushy? Maybe if she just agreed with her, she could ignore her advice and then do what she wanted anyway to get her off her back.

Clara immediately brightened up. "Well, Millie at the Mercantile told me," She began, lowering her voice and conspiratorially whispering behind her hand leaning toward Veronica's ear. "Millie told *me* that Norman's Esther told *her* that this new family has been bidding on the farm next to them and it looks serious that they might take it. It is a family from Canada, moving here because of the milk prices. You heard about the government there changing the dairy laws? No? Well, now all the dairies are required to electrically chill the milk if they want to sell it as Grade A.

The *Amische* there have always used a deep well with the water under forty degrees to meet the health standards, but now they're telling them they can only sell that milk as Grade B for cheese and such. They're losing a ton of money doing that, so some are moving out and *kumming* down here."

"Oh, that's terrible," Veronica agreed while washing another casserole dish.

"Well anyway, Norman's Esther told Millie who told me that they have a bachelor son, talk, dark and handsome, would you believe it? She met them when they brought the county surveyor around to mark the boundaries last week. He looks to be about your age."

Veronica was tiring of Clara's dogged efforts on the subject. She'd become like a broken record. *A thorn in my side,* she told herself. So, to placate Clara she continued, "So how old is this fella?" she asked.

"Well, um, I don't know. But I'll find out for *ya,* okay?" Clara eagerly offered, visibly energized by Veronica's reply.

"Not if it's any trouble, mind you," Veronica said dryly, hoping she wasn't being overly encouraging nor obviously just humoring her.

"Oh!" Clara excitedly answered. "I'll let you know, drop by as soon as I do."

"Well, I don't want you riding all the way to mine, if I might be gone. I do get out, *ya* know, and there's a trip *kumming* up with my single ladies' group," Veronica tried to put off the terrifying possibility of facing Clara in her own kitchen over *kaffi*. She'd never be rid of her then.

Veronica went back to washing the last of the plates, remembering just then the little quote on her inspirational calendar from just that morning. Catherine Doherty had once again hit the nail on the head, wise woman that she was.

"Listening to gossip is participating in it. If there were no listeners, there would be no gossip," it read.

Later that evening at supper, she finished off the last bite of bread and began clearing the table. When all was cleaned up, she again brought out the composition book, turned up the wick slightly in the mantle lamp, sat back down at the table and began to write while thinking to herself, *maybe I will get published someday. Ach! Am I being* brot *or what? Who would want to read this drivel? Maybe I'll get better if I keep at it long enough, though. Who knows?*

Dear Kitty,

We loved that kitchen with its old blue curtains. The addition had a window at both ends of the table. Us kids were always decorating those windows. In Fall we'd make leaf pictures, ironing pretty leaves we'd find between two pieces of wax paper, first putting on a layer of newspaper to iron over, trimming the edges with pinking shears. In winter we made snowflakes out of white paper coffee filters. Christmas cards would be taped up and hung around all the window frames in the house as they arrived. Two kerosene mantle lamps hung from chains from the ceiling over the long table providing all the light we'd need for doing homework in the evenings, though not quite enough light to quilt or darn or mend by. Daytime worked better for those things.

There was a potted bougainvillea plant at each end of the rafter hanging next to the lamp chains which both grew to mammoth proportions, entwining themselves around the chains and the hickory beam between them. You felt like you were in your own private jungle in there. When they flowered, the blooms dripped their perfume down on us below.

If one of us was done with our studies before the others we had to be quiet so as not to interrupt their concentration, but we could sit and write to one of our pen pals or a grossmammi or doddy for an upcoming birthday. If there was a lamb curled up on an old blanket in the crate by the wood stove, I'd take it onto my lap and sit quietly on the floor petting and stroking it and whispering sweet nothings into its ear.

Mamm would check on homework and help wherever she could but most evenings she'd be found by the sink peeling carrots, parsnips, or squash or potatoes and such for the next day's dinner. It would all sit overnight in cold water in the big stainless-steel bowl. Sometimes she'd get out the cast iron Dutch oven and measure dry beans into it, first sorting them to make sure there weren't any tiny pebbles in there, and then pouring in the water. It would sit on the stovetop above the smoldering coals all night. In the morning early, after she put on the coffee and stoked up the fire in the stove again, she'd add molasses, brown sugar, onions, some dry mustard powder, and sometimes a can of tomato paste would go in at this stage, along with some minced bacon or pork scrapple or bits of salt pork. That would bubble away on the stove all morning, starting from before breakfast even, and be ready by dinner time at noon. There'd be a big iron skillet of corn brode still hot from the oven on the right side of the wood stove. Mamm would cover the corn brode with a towel as soon as it came out of the oven to make it sweat so it wouldn't dry out. The table would be set with butter and a pitcher of hot maple syrup, too. I can taste it chust thinking about it.

Some evenings after supper she would start up a new jar of sprouts from alfalfa or broccoli seeds or make a sponge for baking brode the next morning from the sourdough starter that lived in the warming oven above the stove on the right side, away from any draughts. Dat would be reading The Budget mostly, putting it down only when Mamm tapped him on the shoulder and silently pointed out with her eyes which one of the younger ones was dozing off and needed carrying upstairs to bed. I realize now that those were the happiest times of my life, but I didn't know that then, only trying my darnedest to grow up fast and be all growed up, as we said.

Without telephones or access to computers and email, the next best way to keep in touch with all our friends and relatives out there and hear anything else newsworthy was to read The Budget. Of course, we'd all write lots of circular letters with each one adding their own two cents to it before sending it on to the next reader listed on the back of the envelope. We'd have circle letters chust for our girlfriends, too, back then. All the latest gossip, though we were constantly admonished not to gossip. Especially during your teen years, you want to share all those exciting things that are going on. A new family moving into the district with a whole handful of the most oh-so-gut-looking sons ever! Or a skating party for the youngie, and who had a new sled pulled by a whole team. Or who you saw at the singing and who drove you home and how your heart absolutely stopped! Those teen years were the best. I was absolutely oblivious to anything else. I thought that our whole life was heaven on earth. The ministers called it 'The Ark,' like we were chosen to be separate and thus saved, while the rest of the world was on a collision course and would self-destruct through their own sin. I was so very naïve. I didn't have a clue. I chust assumed my teen years would be one big youngie party, dreaming of marrying, giving names to all my children, even writing lists of my favorite baby names in my diary. It never crossed my mind that it could be anything but rosy.

In this dream world no one died, babies were always born perfect, and husbands were never controlling or angry or drunk, which would land them in the Bann thus getting the whole family shunned. There were no miscarriages, no buggy accidents. Nothing that could rip your heart in two. The rest of my life should be wunderbar-gut. I never doubted that. It was chust assumed. There were no other options in my deluded mind back then. I was *not prepared for the real world for sure. These days I hardly read at all, though. I am floating between despair and blatant resignation sometimes, when I stop to take stock, as if I don't have any choice in the matter, which I don't believe I do. My life has been decided for me. Is this how it shall be till I die? All the years ahead spread out, spent dragging through each day, wishing it all over with? Sad. I don't write much some days.* Chust *this trash. Feeling sorry for myself. But I can't shake it no matter how hard I try. And I don't believe I really want someone named Henry in the mix.*

She made a mental note then to erase the last few lines. She closed the notebook and leaving everything on the table, turned down the knob on the kerosene lamp and blew out the wick before heading upstairs. She could write tomorrow. Maybe she'd get some happier insights by then.

She said her prayers, kneeling by her bed. Then her thoughts floated back to a letter she had received long ago, about a year after Amos had been taken from her. This one was not from Henry. It was a few years before him. She still prayed for its sender every night. It continued to puzzle her. It up-ended everything she had assumed about the world and the *Englischers* who peopled it.

The day had started like every other day. Well, not exactly. It was the first anniversary of her husband's death. It had been quite a year. That was already seven years ago now. Still, it seemed like yesterday. The entire Amish community had risen to the occasion those long seven years ago and surrounded her with love and care beyond her wildest dreams. And that support had not dwindled nor stopped in all this time. She sold the cows eventually to downsize the farm to a manageable holding. She kept the two sheep and the chickens and let the ducks and geese decide if they wanted to stay, which it appeared they did, always returning from their expeditions into the surrounding fields and woods by day. The barn cats turned feral which suited her and her neighbors just fine. They were happy to attend to the mice population at the farms in the area. Food was still being dropped off at her back door whenever folks drove by in their buggies to wherever they were going. After the meal on church Sundays, the women in the kitchen always pressed Tupperware containers on her, filled with the good leftover fare to take home. Then they would add a cake or pie, or even both, to the pile. She often didn't have to cook much during the week at all.

Life was returning to what she would describe as 'the new normal' as the next year wore on. The worst of the depression was behind her, though she was completely compliant and took the pills the doctor had prescribed. She might not have to take them forever, but she was grateful for them, not wanting to ever return to that black abyss she found herself in right after the accident. She often included the doctor who'd invented the magic pills in her prayers at night, too, even though she'd never know his name. Before that she had convinced herself that Life had already dished up its worst to her, taking her little baby far too soon. No one should be asked to make a greater sacrifice than that, should they? *Gott* certainly wouldn't give a soul more than it could bear. Of course, He'd give you the grace to carry whatever cross He sent you, right? How many were still telling her that? But then Amos was instantly killed when that fancy car ran the stop sign that fateful night, and her world and all she thought she believed in was turned upside down and inside out. Until nothing...made...sense.

But a year later it was beginning to. And then one day she walked down to the mailbox as she watched the mailman pulling his little truck away. As always, she pulled out a bundle of junk mail, which always made her wonder where all the junk mail from the whole country went to. All into town dump sites? At least the Amish could use it up for kindling. Such a waste though, and she doubted most would even read all of it.

The letter was thick enough not to get lost inside all the advertisements. She was puzzled, reading the return address on the official-looking envelope.

"Huh," she said out loud to herself. "Attorneys at Law. Dallas, Texas. Whatever?"

Once she was back in the kitchen, she sat down and ripped open the letter. It was written, typed actually, very formally cloaked in all sorts of legal language, but at the end was one sentence she could understand:

"... thus, now upon completion of these legal approvals, it is concluded that $1,000,000 will be granted to the beneficiary, Veronica Schwartz, which will be deposited into the U.S. Bank in her name in her county of residence, therein to accrue interest as long as it applies, and said funds exist. Signed...."

"This can't be right," she said out loud. "Is this a prank? That's it. But who? Why?"

"It can't be real," she concluded. She'd take it to the minister and find out what it was all about.

The minister and his wife lived only a mile away, so after *redding* up her horse and putting on her travel bonnet, she headed over there. She questioned the meaning of the letter during the entire ride to the minister's house. Tying up her horse to a shade tree in the yard, she practically ran up to the kitchen door and called out announcing her arrival while opening it. The minister's wife was in the kitchen cleaning up after their lunch.

"*Kumm* in," she welcomed Veronica. "*Sits ana.*"

Her husband wandered in to see who his wife was talking to.

"Well, how are you, Veronica? It's *gut* to see you," he said extending his hand.

"I brought this to you to sort out for me," she hurried on to tell him, while still untying the ribbons on her black travel bonnet. "I can't imagine what it is about, mind you," she explained, handing him the envelope as they sat down at the table in the expansive kitchen. "It could *chust* be a prank. I don't know, one of those scams you hear about...."

While the minister's wife silently set a mug of coffee and a generous slice of chocolate mocha jelly roll before Veronica without even asking if she was hungry, the minister carefully unfolded the letter. Opening it he began to read it silently to himself, slowly flipping through the pages. Then he reread it once more from the beginning. Finally, he spoke.

"Well, well, uh, I think it says that you have been named on this check for, *eh,*" at this he coughed before he could say more. Clearing his throat once again he went on. "One million dollars. *Gut Gott!*" he finally exclaimed, looking up at Veronica and then at his wife.

"But why? Who is it from?" she stammered.

"Well, what I can make out is that it is from..." here he flipped the pages back to the beginning and read, "'the estate of the late Leroy Smith.' Now the only time I've heard that name was after your *halsband's* accident. I think this fellow was driving the car that ran the red light. He was pretty badly injured but survived. Elderly man. His family owns that old historic stone house, over by Esopus Creek. It's a pretty fancy place, in the family for over two hundred years, I hear tell.

His wife's name is Dorothy." He sat there thinking. Finally, he said, "Maybe we should drive over there and see what we can find out, *eh?*" he asked, looking up at her, his raised eyebrows colluding with the question. Veronica nodded in agreement.

"Let's finish dessert first," his wife suggested. "Then we can go down there and see what this is all about, maybe."

CHAPTER 14
Ruth & Veronica

R uth arrived unannounced, once again. Veronica heard the horse clip-clopping up the drive this time and jumped up from the table, darting to the kitchen window to see who it might be. Again, it was in the middle of her breakfast. She'd grabbed her starched *kapp* up from the table where it sat in case her visitor was someone like a minister's or bishop's wife whom she should show more respect for, and she would have plopped it on over her bun then, but saw it was Ruth who didn't count in that category, so it was set back down on the checkered tablecloth.

"Well, hello there," Veronica called out from the back doorway. "What brings you here this early?"

Ruth reached into the back of the buggy and brought out a large purse. "I wanted to go over some of my charting with you so you could learn how to do it," she explained as she followed Veronica back into the kitchen.

"*Kaffi?*" Veronica offered.

"*Ya. Denki.* I'll never turn down *kaffi.*"

Sitting at the table, Ruth spread out the folders, while Veronica brought the two mugs to the table setting them down next to a half-pint Mason jar filled with camel milk before she sat down next to Ruth.

"Now this is how we chart labor, on the first white page," she explained. "Each *mamm* has a folder with her name on this tab," Ruth began, pointing out the tab. "Hour by hour we write down any progression, anything unusual, blood pressure, and temperature, even if she is *chust* resting."

"Okay, I see," Veronica agreed, *though I don't have a clue what any of that means,* she told herself.

"Now if I ask you to write down anything, you'll know where it is," Ruth added.

"Now these pages here on the blue page are each a prenatal visit. We'll do a few in the district today so you can see how that's done."

Veronica nodded.

"Then these pages—the pink pages—are for notes. I write down my impressions after I leave each visit. If the *mamm* seems unusually tired or has a poor appetite—anything, I can ask about that at the next visit and follow it up or even have her come into the clinic to be checked. I can't do labs out in the field but if I suspect a UTI or other infection or something I have to get the doctor involved in it anyway so he can write a prescription," Ruth continued. "Then the doctor can clear her so I can follow her again. If the problem persists he may want to have a hospital birth, then, and we'll put together a plan for that."

"Wow, I didn't know it was all so technical," Veronica said.

"And this last one, the light green page is for the baby. We assess how he or she is doing after birth—it's called an 'Apgar Score.' And we continue to check them both post-partum and enter that here, too. Well, it's important that we don't assume we know what we are looking at—ever, and that we don't miss anything either. We want it to be super safe and be able to have a *gut* outcome. Take Mavis here," Ruth said as she pulled out another file. Opening it up she pointed to a tan page labeled 'LABS.' "She's been persistently anemic, and the doctor is having her come in for iron shots now. If it goes untreated, she could be at risk of hemorrhaging."

"Mm. I see," Veronica said, *though I don't see at all. Not a bit. It's all Greek to me,* she told herself, and then asked Ruth, "You aren't scared of making a mistake?"

"That's why it takes so many years of training, so we know what we can and are allowed to manage and what is outside of our scope of practice. We are trained over and over and *over* again to see what *normal* birth is, so that when a red flag does go up, you are instantly on it. You'll never get any respect from the wider medical community if you come in all confident and know-it-all. Arrogant. This work requires that you are constantly humble and respectful. I haven't prayed so much or so hard in all my life as I do at a birth. You'll see. It is an awesome responsibility but then it is a huge honor too. A sacred honor. Have you got anymore *kaffi?*" Ruth asked.

"*Ya,* let me get it," Veronica offered popping up from the table.

"That's still that Amish camel milk?" Ruth wanted to know. "I really like it. I'm surprised. Amazing what a body can get used to."

"*Ya,* I am super happy I discovered it," Veronica said.

Ruth started returning the folders back into her bag and wrapped her hands around the coffee mug. "Anything else going on here?" she wanted to know.

"Well," Veronica began slowly. "I have a widower up in Canada writing to me every other week now. I *chust* don't know. I really don't think I could go through all that again, *ya* know. Losing a *halsband,* burying a *bobbel....*" The room became still then. Only the soft crackles from the wood stove could be heard.

"How did she die?" Ruth asked gently.

"Well," Veronica hesitated, looking down into her mug. She had shared the details with very few outside her immediate family. She still didn't want to remember all that once again.

"She came much too early. They knew there were problems before she was even born. She stayed so tiny. They did a bunch of tests and then sent me to a specialist—a neonatologist—who said she wouldn't make it through the delivery and offered to terminate the pregnancy before I was even six months along. It was *baremlich*. We said there was no way we'd do that. He listed all the things that it could be, what could go wrong: Trisomy, Downs, Congenital Heart Defects, IUGR—Intrauterine Growth Retardation they called it--but we didn't care about all that. We tried so hard to trust the Lord and the prayers of the church. It was so hard," Veronica said as she pulled a handkerchief out of her sleeve.

"Oh, I am so sorry," Ruth said as she reached out and covered Veronica's hand with her own.

"She lived only three days in the hospital. On the third day I asked them why she was on a respirator. They explained that it was breathing for her. I asked what would happen if they took it out. They said she couldn't breathe on her own then. Well, I had a think about that. *Ya* know, when you love your *bobbel* that much, you *chust* can't see them suffering, so we both agreed, Amos and I, and told them to take it out. I held her then. And that was it. She would be almost seven now."

Ruth's tears were falling now too.

"I can't have anymore *kinner*. I *chust* can't. I couldn't bear to go through that again. I'd crack up...be no *gut* to anybody," Veronica whispered.

"Have you ever gone back to ask why? If it was something hereditary?" Ruth tentatively asked.

"No. Why would I? It could happen again, couldn't it?" Veronica asked with obvious surprise.

"Not if it wasn't genetic. There is a grant in the country here *chust* now that I can refer you to for testing. It would be free. I've sent one couple there already. They had the same kind of questions. Let me know if you'd like to get some answers, okay? It might put your mind at rest," Ruth offered.

Ruth headed outside as she tied her bonnet, while Veronica rinsed out the mugs and checked the wood stove. She clipped on her *kapp,* carefully fitting her black travelling bonnet on over it and tied the ribbons below her chin. She continued to think about what Ruth had just suggested. Finding out more. It had never occurred to her. They could figure this stuff out? Actually? Did she really want to go into all that again?

They were going to visit some of the *mamms* in the area. Some were due soon and others had recently had their babies. Ruth explained what a follow-up visit entailed as she steered her horse down the drive and onto the shoulder of the road.

"So, we've put together a check list of all the things you should ask about or observe on a prenatal visit, and also a follow-up postnatal visit. That way when you are learning you kind of have a cheat sheet, so you don't forget anything," Ruth explained as they arrived at the first farm on their list. They directed the horse up near the house and hopped out of the buggy.

"I won't unhitch her since this is *chust* a follow-up visit," Ruth said handing Veronica a file folder. "This won't take long. Why don't you check off each thing as we talk about it, *eh?*"

"You'll tell me where I am on the page if I get lost?" Veronica wanted to know.

"Sure," Ruth agreed as she tied the horse to the hitching post. "You'll be able to do it all in your sleep come this time next year," Ruth chuckled.

"I doubt that, if I don't get fired before then," Veronica said under her breath as she began untying her black bonnet and followed behind Ruth.

CHAPTER 15

Rambouillet & Romneys

Veronica was dropped off at home later that day. It was fun meeting the new babies and their *mamms*. It left her with plenty of thoughts, though. She could not have imagined this in her wildest dreams. *I would feel so terrible if anything ever went wrong. Best leave this to the experts,* she told herself. *Ruth seems so confident. She is so gut with the* mamms. *You can tell they trust her, too.*

Veronica put her purse down on a kitchen chair and removed her traveling bonnet and white *kapp*. She sat down and took off her shoes and stockings. *Time to do some chores,* she thought to herself as she grabbed her old, steel-gray chore apron off a peg and then the egg basket in the mud room on her way out. Heading for the *kesselhaus* and reaching under a sleepy hen for eggs, she saw again the beautiful baby they had visited today. She sighed deeply. *If only my little one had lived. They are so helpless. You want to do anything for them, you'd love them forever.* Those pesky tears again made an appearance. *Why me? I could have had a houseful by now if Amos hadn't died. I'd be run ragged and the happiest person on earth. Oh, why me? And I can't have even one...healthy...* At that she sniffed and rummaged through her apron pocket for her hankie.

The free-range chickens still needed to be rounded up for the night. The ducks and geese needed to be herded into their penned yard. Then she checked that the sheep hadn't wandered too far and had plenty of clover and alfalfa hay, fresh corn and grain mix, and clean straw in their open hut. Without cows her chores took practically no time at all. Her horse was already in the barn. She'd let him out into the paddock that morning and found him by the barn door when she came home. She had mucked out the stall before breakfast and filled his feed box then, too.

Before breakfast that morning she'd put on a pot of salsify soup and stoked up the fire in the stove. She set the egg basket down next to the sink and washed her hands, scrubbing with the little brush. Turning and walking toward the stove she lifted the lid on the blue Dutch oven. Steam rose up telling her the soup was plenty hot. She had grown several rows of the salsify, a parsnip-like vegetable last summer. It held up quite well in the root cellar over the winter. Known also as the oyster plant, these giant 'pencils' are members of the dandelion family, a Mediterranean plant with a delicate taste, ever so slightly sweet, some say slightly reminiscent of oyster. Many liken it to an artichoke instead. They can also be roasted.

The Hobo bread was still on the table from that morning, wrapped up in a tea towel and the little crock of camel milk butter sat next to it, along with the sweet Amish peanut butter spread. She was trying mightily to cut back on sugar, but the spread was just too good to do without. One part peanut butter and one part store bought whipped marshmallow fluff must have been the bane of many an Amish mother trying to shed a few pounds. The bread's slightly sweet flavor would certainly go well with the soup. It wasn't quite dusk yet, too early to light the mantle lamp over the kitchen table. Maybe in half an hour she'd want it. She walked around the kitchen closing the windows and the curtains there. Veronica stirred the creamy soup with the ladle and filled a bowl. As she sat down, she had another thought. It was still early in the evening so she would have all the hours ahead to write before she headed to bed. Reaching across the table she snatched up her composition book lying on the tablecloth and the pencils sitting by it. She reread the last pages she'd written so she could add to the story from there. She had to do at least something productive and not just sit feeling sorry for herself all evening. The picture of that perfect precious baby was still in her thoughts, though.

Dear Kitty,

Avram married first, which I guess is how it should be, him being the oldest. Felicity is a dear. They are really so happy, even after over a decade now. I've never seen them not happy. They have kinner *who are strong and healthy and another* bobbel *on the way, which is obvious to me, but then no one is supposed to know. At least we don't talk about such private things and certainly not in front of the children. For that matter, if anyone asks when you are due, the pat answer in Plain circles, at least, is 'time will tell,' as in, 'it isn't any of your business, anyway.' Kind of old fashioned to my thinking. But then there is so much gossip that goes around all the time at sewing bees and such that some* mamms *even try not to gain any weight at all and then one day they* kumm *home with a* bobbel *and surprise everyone. In my opinion, that is plain stupid.* Gott *gives us this incredible, precious miracle and we think we have to hide it. I wonder if that's why we have too many fragile newborns. I don't see too many hearty ones, not enough at least. I used to think it was because* mamms *worked too hard. Maybe that is why I grew up so clueless. Everything always seemed so perfect. I was never told much about death, though it happened on the farm to the animals. We took that for granted. Old people died and we had a wake and us children were brought along so we got to see the* grossmammi *or* doddy *lying there all dressed in white in a plain coffin up on two sawhorses in their living room, candles everywhere. I didn't mind going to wakes. If I sat real quiet and didn't wiggle while my parents visited in whispers with all the other parents then I got to go through the kitchen afterwards and fill my apron pocket with cookies and eat them all in the back of the buggy on the way home. Like a consolation prize for being good. My older sister Tamar clued me in to the proper etiquette at wakes in order to get cookies. She sat me down one night on her bed and told me all about it. There were always trays piled high with them. Probably all the* mamms *got busy baking when they'd heard someone died. Sometimes there were bowls of store-bought candy, too. Jolly Ranchers if we got super lucky.*

Tamar married next. There was some drama going on about having to put the wedding off or something, but Mamm *would never explain it to me, and in the end, they did get married and seemed* chust *fine then. I did see them* shmunzling *out in the barn once, which I thought wasn't allowed until after they were married. At least that was a topic that came up several times a year in the sermons at church. They were sure going at it. Then he took her hand and led her up to the hay loft. I left then. I* chust *got a funny feeling that I shouldn't be there. That started me thinking about all that then. I guess I wanted to be liked like that someday. When I was a teacher, I once got a book at the library and read it in between the stacks, in secret. For certain I wasn't going to bring* that *book home. That sure opened my eyes. I didn't know the half of it, before then. I guessed, in the end though, that if* Gott *created man and woman and declared that it was 'very* gut,' *then it must be okay.*

She took up a fresh pencil and continued from there.

Rufus was next in line. He wasn't in a hurry to get hitched. He was a hard worker and was super obedient to Dat *and* Mamm, *but when the subject came up, he'd* chust *josh and say he was born to be a bachelor. He played hard too, riding bareback, swimming in lakes, hiking mountains with friends. One year he built* Mamm *a proper pizza oven out back of the kitchen. He'd done all the research on them and got it pretty perfect I'd say, lining it with clay tiles on the inside. If it had been stoked up hot enough, then after the pizzas came out,* Mamm *could still put a cake in there and it would cook that too with the heat left from the pizzas. In his teens, he and* Dat *built the summer kitchen* chust *behind the house. It was basically a roof over a cement slab without walls, like a gazebo, big enough for a wood stove and a couple of tables. The breeze coming through there was so* gut *on a hot day when you were canning or butchering chickens. You didn't have to heat up the whole house during the summer or fall when you were canning all day. Before we had the summer kitchen, the heat from downstairs would rise when* Mamm *canned or baked or had the wood stove running all day, and you could hardly sleep upstairs those nights it was so hot.*

Rufus is the one that got Dat *onto the sheep. He calculated that we'd make more money selling fleeces from specialty sheep, like Rambouillet and Romneys, and they ate less than cows and could stay out longer in the fall and took up less room in the barns besides. We could also package and sell mutton. No one else in the district had sheep at that time and we could sell the meat easily. Lots of folks liked it. He could sell it at the farmers' markets, and it always sold out.*

Rufus started going to singings again somewhere in there, back then. I'd known he was seeing some girl pretty regularly when he started taking long baths and sneaking some aftershave every Saturday night. I could smell it a mile away. I was happy for him. He eventually married Suzy and they are still really happy to this day. Nothing bad ever happened to any of them. I wouldn't wish that on anyone, but I do wonder why I seem to always get a whop-

ping share of whatever life could and did throw at me. I can't imagine why, if somehow I attract troubles. Like a magnet. What if Gott doesn't send us the troubles at all? What if that is chust all life is, that Adam's fall threw us into a new era where Nature and the rest of the world is chust like this and Gott is chust there to be by our side through it all? Maybe, chust maybe, Gott isn't the original puppeteer pulling all the strings, knowing what the rest of our lives will look like... what every minute will hold.

Enough grappling for one day, she told herself as she gathered up the things on the table. *It's time to get ready for tomorrow. Church Sunday. Maybe lay out an outfit chust in case Ruth calls.* "Whatever next?" she said out loud to herself, taking up the flashlight by the kitchen door and heading out to the outhouse just a few steps away.

Part Two

"*Do not ask the Lord to guide your footsteps if you are not willing to move your feet.*"

— AMISH PROVERB

CHAPTER 16

Dancing Pigs

After church the *fraus* all headed for the big farmhouse kitchen to help out with lunch. The men and boys would eat first. Then, when they get up, the girls will dash in with wash basins of soapy hot water and filled basins with plain hot water for rinsing and then dry and set the places once again--all right at the tables. Then the older women and *mamms* will eat while the girls keep the babies happy. Then the rest will descend on the tables once more after the second clean-up and eat whatever is still left, which there is usually enough of, though the ends of the loaves of bread might be all that's left of that, and they'll scrape out the bottom of the soup kettle and the salad bowls. No one will starve though what with all the pies and cakes and cobblers and bars that have come along and then there's less to bring back home anyway.

Veronica gazed out over the lawn. It was a gorgeous spring day. Perfect for having lunch outside. In the winter it got rather squished serving everyone indoors, even if the walls did fold away to open up the whole downstairs floor space for the tables. This was so much more relaxing. The *kinner* could chase and run to their hearts' content, barefoot for sure, by the end of March if not sooner. Groups of little boys were heading for the barns to check out the horses and buggies there. They knew the teenagers on this farm had built themselves courting buggies and it was a favorite topic of conversation among themselves, what kind they would have when they grew up. They would try to impress each other with tidbits of knowledge they'd gleaned from the latest horse auction they'd accompanied their *dats* to.

Teenage girls were huddled by the vegetable garden chatting with their friends. They were already finished with eighth grade, so they didn't get to see their friends every day any longer. Careful not to gossip, they nevertheless needed to share all the latest news garnered since the last church Sunday two weeks prior. A group of grade school girls sat under a large sprawling tree in the yard playing with the babies and toddlers they had been assigned, imagining they were *mamms* and wondering if their own eventual offspring would be as adorable or fussy or contrary as these. Any newborns were being nursed in one of the upstairs bedrooms where their *mamms* were exchanging recipes for curing colic or thrush or cradle cap or agreeing or disagreeing about how long to let a baby cry at night.

Veronica was sitting with the other women who had been serving the meal. Now they were the last to eat so there was no pressure to hurry to make room for anyone else. Hazel came by with a large coffee pot to refill their cups, followed by her niece Henrietta who was all of ten years old, carefully carrying a carton of half and half in one hand and a sugar bowl in the other.

"Well, this is service! *Denki*," Veronica said as the pair topped off her coffee mug.

"I wRuth be a waitress in one of them fancy restaurants when I growed up," the girl offered.

"Oh my!" Veronica replied. "I would think there'd be better jobs to aspire to, perhaps."

"Well, if I can't do that, then I want to be a ballerina or a vest-er-in-air-ian," the serious little girl assured her with a nod. "I have a book from the li-berry about a girl pig who gets to be a ballerina," the chatty child continued as she attempted to stand on her tiptoes.

"Whoa, there," her aunt cautioned. "You can do that when you're not serving the cream, missy." Then her aunt Hazel laughed out loud and shook her head before moving on to the next coffee mug down the table while gently guiding her little charge by her free hand on the girl's shoulder.

Matilda was sitting on the other side of Veronica. She looked forward to church Sunday every other week because it was often the only time she got out of the busy house where she was a *maud* and could have a decent conversation with other adults.

"As soon as Franny and I got the chocolates made and in the icebox full with enough for two weeks' worth of farmers' markets and that wedding order sent off, wouldn't *ya* know I'd get asked to be a *maud* again. I don't mind a'tall, but I'm not getting any younger, don't *ya* know? They *chust* had their tenth. She's not gettin' any younger either, and it isn't so easy anymore. She *chust* wasn't bouncing back like she did with the others. Finally, her *halsband* got ahold of the midwife and had her *kumm* out and check her out. *Gut* thing he did, too. She was anemic, really low iron. Pretty bad, too. She is finally starting to perk up, but we try to let her rest as much as possible. I've been making her some *gut* iron foods like lentil soup and fruit soup, too. I sent him to the co-op with a list and he got all sorts of things for her. I put a bunch of kale in the lentil soup, and prunes, apricots, and raisins in the fruit soup. I also give her black strap molasses tea all day, a *gut* dollop in each cup."

"Is that all that goes in it? I never made that, fruit soup," Veronica cut in.

"No, I put apricots, dates, figs, prunes, raisins, a little cut-up lemon, a cinnamon stick, some whole dry cloves, honey if you like, or a little brown sugar. You simmer it covered. I do it overnight on a warm stove with *chust* enough water to cover the fruit. I've been giving it to her over yogurt. The *kinner* sure like it, too. I figure it's gotta be *gut* for growing *kinner,* also. My *mamm* swore by it when us girls got our monthlies. She taught me a lot, she did," Matilda continued. "Well, she's got those *kinner* working alright. She runs a tight ship as they say. I don't have to gather up the wash or put away the dishes and all. They do that. I *chust* have to keep it all running, plan the meals, get the boys to haul the hot water, send one out to the chickens, another to chop some tinder, the girls can sweep, even the littler ones. And they *kumm* when I call them. I don't have to keep hollering at all. But boy, am I ready for bed at the end of the day, for sure."

"Well, I've got some news," Veronica ventured.

"Is he *kumming* to visit? When?" Matilda jumped with excitement.

"No," Veronica chuckled. "We're still writing, and I am not ready for that yet. Not at all."

"Well, what is it then?" Matilda pressed on.

"So, Ruth Lapp is midwifing now. She's gotten her state certification and all. She showed up the other day—was I ever shocked—asking if I'd help her when she needs an assistant. She doesn't want to go solo she says, doing a birth at home alone, and she'll teach me along the way. I really don't know if I'm cut out for this, *ya* know. I'm scared I'll do something wrong, or the baby will have some trouble for sure. I *chust* don't know, Matilda," she said, reaching out to put her hand over Matilda's. "What would you do?" Veronica pleaded with her eyes.

"Oh, my! I don't know," Matilda replied taking Veronica's hand. "I never thought about it. I'd be scared stiff, I think."

"Well, I am for certain," Veronica said. "She came by again after that and brought me a pager that I carry around so she can call me or beep me or something when she is on the way to pick me up to go to a birth. I never saw one before."

"You never seen a pager?" Matilda inquired.

"No, silly. I've never seen a birth," Veronica corrected her. "My *mamm* always farmed us all out and my own was so horrible with all the problems and I was out of it, to be honest." Veronica opened her purse just enough for Matilda to look down into it and see the pager for herself.

"Yikes. I didn't see that *kumming*," Matilda said. "I think I'd pray a whole lot more if I was doing that kinda work."

"Yeah. I do. I got enough to pray for into the next century, for certain. See, I can't even die then, I got so much going on." Veronica laughed wryly. "Like that gospel song, 'Ain't Got Time to Die, So Busy Serving My Lord....' I do, pray all the time, and now asking *Gott* to find someone else for him, Henry, the fellow who keeps writing." Veronica said shaking her head and scoffing once again at the ludicrous idea, first of being an assistant midwife and then the possibility of remarrying.

Just then Matilda spied another old friend. "You gotta excuse me, Veronica. I see Jake's Norma over there," she said as she jumped up from the bench. "I haven't seen her since forever," she expained and was quickly off. At practically the same moment, Clara sat down next to her. *Was she waiting for a chance to interrogate me? I wouldn't put it past her,* Veronica thought, shaking her head slightly. *Be charitable, now,* she chided herself, pasting on a smile that she hoped wasn't too toothy.

"Why, it's *gut* to see you, Veronica. How've you been keeping?" Clara said, trying to sound especially genuine, seeing as she had her best interests at heart.

"I'm fine." *Now a nice smile, you,* she told herself. "How are you? What have you been up to?" Veronica said, attempting to de-rail the inevitable onslaught she knew was coming and would soon be unleashed.

"Oh, I'm *gut*. Nothing new here. 'Cept I been wanting to tell *ya*," *And here it comes,* Veronica mused to herself as Clara rattled on, "...all about this widower I heard tell. I went to my mother-in-law's church last Sunday, that new district north of here, I'd never been, and she—my mother-in-law—was saying that they *chust* found out from her friend Lucy that her *bruder's frau*, Amy, finally died. She'd been suffering for so long. It was a relief. I can't imagine. Happened last year. But he's got four *kinner*, really sweet ones, two are twins —absolute angels--and they asked me to keep an eye out 'cause he really needs to get a *mamm* for those kids. And I know how much you love children, so I thought of you. A ready-made family, and you could still have some of your own, *ya* know. I told her I know *chust* the *schveshta*. You'd be perfect, eh? I could take you next Sunday if *ya* want...." Clara concluded while holding her breath for an answer with her eyebrows at their highest point. Then Veronica added, to herself, *Uh-huh, right. Little angels with dirty diapers and snotty noses, biting each other...fighting...yeah, right...*

Veronica knew Clara would broach the subject once again, but not this. *A 'ready-made family?' Are you kidding me? Really?* she asked herself. Then reminding herself to be kind to the woman she turned to Clara and smiled as sweetly as she was able to at that moment.

"Oh! Clara," she said. "I am *so* sorry, but I am seeing my friend Ruth next Sunday." It was a little white lie, of course, but Ruth *might* be needing her next Sunday. She could easily get that call on her pager. That much was true. Well, half true.

"Well, it sounds perfect for you. You let me know when you're free then. I imagine he'll be snatched up pretty fast. We don't want to miss this chance either," Clara added. "His name is Felix."

With that Veronica popped up off the bench, grabbed her plate, the crumpled napkin and her mug and excused herself. "We'll be seeing you real soon, Clara," she said, forgetting to paste on the smile this time, desperate to get away. *Is she for real?* She asked herself.

CHAPTER 17

Money & Manure

I t was dusk when Veronica finally hitched up her horse and waved goodbye to the last stragglers at the farm. Barefoot little boys in their Sunday best, which were by now covered in dust, and dirt and grass stains, were still chasing each other around barns and hiding up on top of the outhouse roof only to pounce when one of the others careened around the corner of the barn and failed to look up. Peals of laughter followed, and the race would commence all over again. Picnic tables were being hauled out behind the house, and church benches disassembled once again, to fit perfectly into the back of the bench wagon ready to be driven to the next farm where church would again be conducted in two weeks' time. The last families would be heading to the buggy parking lot, *dats* carrying sleeping babies in their arms to be laid down on a blanket behind the front bench seat, little barefoot dish washers skipping merrily behind them, swinging their shoes by their laces, their bonnets hanging by their strings down their backs.

Pulling the reins to the right Veronica steered the buggy

onto the road's macadam shoulder as she watched the rump of her horse bobbing in rhythm to the clip-clopping on the road below. She relaxed against the bench's short back and gazed over the fields as they passed by.

She couldn't imagine her life any different from this. Church Sundays, friends' get-togethers, pitching in and helping neighbors, writing in the evenings in the quiet of her little home. Why would she need to change any of it? Would this midwifery thing flip her whole world on its tail? A second marriage would for sure. Then there was the whole question of *kinner.* She wouldn't go through that again for all the tea in China. She couldn't. So how should she tell Henry? It will definitely cancel any future with him. It was time to tell him, she decided. Stop fooling around before he got it into his head to visit, maybe even thinking he'd surprise her. At this point it could be taken as leading him on. He was nice and friendly, but children, marriage? No way. Absolutely no way. She had to be honest with him. He at least deserved that. He should be using his time writing to someone else who wanted to get married, not wasting it on her.

Someone who wants to get married. I don't need *to get married, but I've been thinking I don't* want *to get married either. Are they the same thing? No, not really. Hmm. Something to think about....*

The horse bedded down for the night in the barn, she walked back to the house. *It's so quiet here,* she thought to herself. *No kinner, for one. What would that be like? Noise, laughter, fighting, teasing, endless piles of washing, never enough bread made ahead...but would that all be bad?* she thought as she reached the kitchen door. A longing that she had not felt in years hit her in the gut at that moment. It had not crept into her mind since first dating all those years ago. Would she ever feel fulfilled? Really happy? Would she never stop pining for children of her own? She shook her head then as if trying to sweep away all those thoughts. *This isn't helping,* she told herself, opening the screen door to the kitchen.

Veronica kicked off her shoes on the mat, and taking her flashlight checked the wood stove, closed the kitchen windows and lit the lamp over the table. She put her purse down on a chair and covered it with her shawl. Putting a small log into the fire box she checked the damper for the last time. Getting down on her knees she peered under the wood stove to see if she'd caught any mice. The trap was empty. Most mornings it wasn't. Empty. She hated killing the little pests, but it was a necessary evil. The creatures didn't belong in the house.

As she wiggled down into the bed under the fluffy quilt Veronica fell asleep easily enough but then when she woke up in the middle of the night, she realized she was not going to get much more sleep. She tossed and turned and finally lay on her back praying.

So, Gott. *This is the problem. He seems nice enough. He is sincere. He'd make a* gut halsband *for someone, but* chust *not me. I can't imagine You'd ask me to do that. I know I'm not strong enough. Mentally. To bury a* bobbel *and then a* halsband *a year later. I'd crack up for sure if it happened again. Why do that to someone? He doesn't deserve that either. Me, I mean. He doesn't deserve a basket case for a wife. So, I'm thinking I'll tell him and that'll be the end of it and things can go back to normal here.*

Then a thought came. Veronica blinked at the ceiling several times. *Hmmm. I wonder if Ruth might know someone at the clinic who could give me some answers and tell me if all my* kinner *would be born the same. With the same problems. Maybe they could find out from the hospital what exactly went wrong and if all my* bobbeli *would have it. All this time I didn't want to even think I could have healthy* kinner chust *to be horribly disappointed or be unrealistic, or kidding myself that it wouldn't happen again. Hm. Then I'd know for sure one way or th'other if there even is a way to tell. Maybe they'll* chust *say there's a fifty-fifty chance but then I don't think I'd risk that either. Too heart breaking. I'd be a nervous wreck* chust *waiting nine months to find out. No way. I'll ask Ruth though. Who knows?*

Then Veronica could fall back to sleep. She would pursue this, just until she knew one way or the other. If no one could tell her, then she'd assume it could happen again and those statistics were enough to make her decide against tempting fate and choose not to have children. Case closed. She wouldn't have to be wrestling with the subject forever. She could be a happy single woman and move on. She had wallowed in self-pity long enough. Of course, she was depressed. But she didn't have to be. She had years ahead of her. She had her health. She had her church, her single friends and had no reason to dread the future. She could carve out a contented life. Her friends had. With God's help she'd find a way.

Just like He had with the letter from the attorneys. The minister, his wife, and Veronica showed up at the big old colonial stone house later that afternoon. An elderly woman stood in the doorway having heard the horse and buggy coming over the little wooden bridge that crossed the creek, that ran in front of her house. The horse tied up to a tree in the shade, they moved toward the porch. She was tiny, with snow-white hair and a sweet little grin. She waved them into the house as they climbed the front steps. It was dark inside. The interior had been renovated but retained the original style of an old farmhouse. The walls were stone with hickory wood beams along the ceilings. A large wood burning stove was set into a stone alcove in the first room. Antique lamps graced the elaborately carved sideboard. Sconces held kerosene lamps along the outer walls.

They followed the old woman as she made her way into the kitchen. Tapestries hung on some of the walls, and hook and braided rugs were tastefully scattered throughout the house. The kitchen was tidy, they noticed, as she beckoned them to sit at the round oak table there. An ornate lazy Susan graced the center of the table piled high with medicine bottles and little boxes of various preparations, balanced between salt and pepper shakers, a jar of marmalade, and a dish of sugar cubes. An elaborate chandelier with hundreds of antique prisms hung above the table. It had been converted to electricity somewhere along the way and sent a warm glow throughout the room.

Mrs. Smith looked over at the minister then and smiled again. He cleared his throat and began at what he took to be her invitation to speak.

"Well, we have a bit of a puzzle we think perhaps you may be able to help us with. Now, I may be all wrong about that, and I apologize, but we thought we'd start here," he fumbled with the right words before continuing.

"Well, our friend here, Veronica, received a letter that mentions your husband--at least we think it names your husband--but it might be a different Leroy Smith then, we *chust* aren't sure," he continued.

Mrs. Smith nodded then. "Yes, I can explain. I had a hunch you'd be by one of these days," she began. "Yes, he was my husband." Then she turned her gaze to Veronica and continued. "He died a few months after the accident that fatally injured your husband, Amos Schwartz, right?"

Veronica nodded while her eyes teared up once again at the mention of his name, though this still didn't make any sense. Not... at... all.

"Well," the woman continued. "He felt terrible about the

accident. He would relive that day over and over, wondering how he could take it back, or make it right. It haunted him until he died. He was close to ninety then, you know." She paused and looked at the three people across the table from her before continuing.

"Well, he died peacefully, at least. Our pastor suggested we include you in his will. It would be the least we could do. Now we had plenty of life insurance, and I've recently sold the property here. I got top dollar for the land alone. And the house is historic-listed. I am moving in with one of my daughters next month. I don't need such a big place and it's getting harder to live alone. The windows will need replacing soon, and there are hundreds of other things I'd need to repair or update. Between the will and the house I don't have to tell you how well set up we are. He'd inherited quite a lot of family wealth, too. Leroy finalized the will just weeks before he died. He left everything to me which our children will divide when I'm gone. I am eighty-seven, though it's hard to believe, really. Four million dollars will go four ways, and the extra million from the life insurance is rightfully going to you, my dear. You must accept it. I promised him you would. The old fool should have given up driving long ago. He knew that, but what old person gives up their pride?" she quipped, the regret evident in her voice. After another moment she added quite cheerily, "Lemonade anyone?"

"Oh my...oh my!" Veronica said. "That is too much, really, I never expected..."

"Don't worry," the old lady cut in. "We know you will use it wisely. It is a gift. You and your family can live comfortably, and you can help others in your community, too. We understand you Amish don't carry health or life insurance, right? I wish we could undo the past, that your husband never had that accident, but we can't. We must make our lives mean something in the aftermath of that. This is what we decided, together, both of us."

Veronica looked down at her hands as she nervously twisted the corner of her apron. Shaking her head, she looked up at the minister.

"But we can't keep the money, can we?" Veronica asked. "I mean we don't sue people for damages and all, right? And this is sort of like that?"

Dorothy Smith answered the question before the minister could. "No, it is not like that. It is a gift, giving back for all we have been given," nodding her head to emphasize her point. "Leroy used to quote Dolly Levi who once said," she continued, "'money is like manure. It's no good unless it's spread around.'"

CHAPTER 18
Calling It Quits

Dear Henry,

Greetings in our dear Lord's name!

I have been pretty busy here and haven't written in a while. Hope you and Rosie are well. The gardens are pretty perky, chust *now. We'll be canning soon enough. The single* fraus' *group went on a* wunderbar *outing last week. We had a* gut *time. I always enjoy seeing them and seeing new places. We get talking about everything, ya know. I heard that it's getting harder and harder to find* gut *schoolteachers out our way here. I don't know if I'd be up to that again. It's for sure been a long time since I taught school. Families keep having* kinner *and the* Amische *schools are getting bigger, and they have to split some districts so they don't get too big, but then they'll need two teachers come fall.* Chust *some trivia here from my reading. I know, I keep gathering all these facts. It doesn't help anyone, really.* Chust *interesting. So here is what I read: There were approximately 300,000 of us* Amische *in the U.S. in the beginning of the 21*[st] *Century according to a study done at the Elizabethtown College in Pennsylvania. They say a reasonable presumption would be that the Amish population doubles every 15 to 30 years. In other words, every generation is about twice as big as the one before it. Even with some* Amische *youth leaving, that means the average woman must be having about six or seven* kinner. *We know many who have more than that.*

The biggest news is that my friend, Ruth, has asked me to go with her as an assistant for her midwifery work. For certain I didn't see that one kumming. *Not at all. She set me up with a pager so she can let me know the driver is on the way to pick me up. We checked in with some of the* mamms *the other day. I don't think I was cut out for this, though. I might* chust *help her out for a while.* Chust *till she finds a more permanent apprentice. She can only attend low risk births, so she usually doesn't have any trouble. If something else is going on, the* mamm *has to connect with a local hospital for her care. Well, anyway, I will keep you posted on this latest adventure. I don't think I have the nerves for it though.*

I've been thinking here quite a bit. I've come to the conclusion that I need to share some things with you. You seem really nice. An honest, Gott*-fearing* gut *man. But basically, it feels like I am* chust *leading you on. I really don't want to do that, and it isn't fair to you. You should be getting to know someone who really does want to be married and I am sure there is no shortage of eligible* fraus *in all of Canada. The other thing is that our first baby died. She was born much too early and had all sorts of problems. Any other children I'd have could very well have the same problems. So, any more children are out of the picture, for me too. So, there it is. It doesn't look very* gut *for your prospects. I couldn't go through that again, either. You'd have quite a basket case on your hands then, and you'd be stuck with me besides. Not exactly a cheerful marriage. So, I am suggesting we break it off with that and keep each other's intentions in our prayers. I only wish you well.*

Friend Veronica

CHAPTER 19
Seeing Angels

After her shopping was done in the little town, Veronica untied her horse from the hitching rail outside of Millie's quilt store and climbed up onto the buggy's bench. Sitting down, a thought occurred to her. Pennelope. She'd stop in and see how her dear aunt was doing. She had plenty to tell. It had been four weeks since she'd last seen her.

Pennelope lived across the district a good forty minutes' drive away, but it was still morning, and an absolutely lovely day besides. Pennelope also lived alone, but she was in the *dawdy haus,* the little extension off the main farmhouse where her son and his growing family lived. Widowed ten years ago, she'd raised her brood in this house. When the last one flew the nest, she was left alone. It only made sense that her oldest take over the big house and the farm. He'd been renting his house down the road, and this house had been paid for decades earlier. His house would be snatched up within days, should he put it up for rent or sale. There was by no means a glut of housing on arable farmland in the area. Some young couple would certainly grab at the opportunity.

Pulling up to the farm and parking in the shade, she climbed down and tied up the horse to a fence there. She stopped to survey the beautifully kept farm. There were flowers everywhere. The clothes lines were filled with the day's wash. Tiny shirts, small colorful pastel dresses and little barn door trousers were neatly lined up in rows. The cloth Birdseye diapers, however, dominated the yard. *Like flags flying on a hill,* Veronica thought to herself. *The big house must have another* bobbel, she mused. *I'll never have that opportunity,* she told herself while she walked up to the back door. *Stop that right now!* she ordered her thoughts. *Why can't I* chust *get on with it? It's been long enough for sure,* she admonished herself.

She walked around to the side of the house to where Pennelope lived and knocked on the door. As she untied her travel bonnet, she opened the door into the tidy little kitchen. It was smaller than her own house. *Almost like a doll house,* she thought. *So sweet! And some little person has brought her flowers,* she laughed to herself, noticing a fistful of thoroughly wilted wildflowers that sat in a jar of water in the center of the little table. A few pictures were taped to the wall by the stove, obviously masterpieces executed by unnamed miniature artists, at least first grade artists, rendered in crayons. Here was an attempt at drawing a horse. This one looked like a flock of ducks, and another was clearly the artist's family, lined up from smallest to the larger members. There was even a dog sitting by one of the depictions of a child. It made Veronica sad thinking she would never have a little one bringing home pictures for her. Just then Pennelope came in the door.

"Oh, I thought that was your buggy. I was over in the big house holding the *bobbel* while Ruthmarie took a bath. So *gut* to see you!"

"Well," Veronica began. "I knew you were home by your buggy. It isn't too often you see a buggy with plastic daisies tied on, *eh?* It's actually a genius idea. I think I'll get some plastic violets or roses for mine. It takes forever to find my buggy in a field after church or a *frolic,* for certain."

"No, that's for sure," Pennelope replied. "What are you doing today?"

"Well, I finished my errands, and it was *chust* too beautiful a day to go straight home. You busy?" she asked.

"No. Not at all. I'm glad for the company. Here, *sits ana,*" Pennelope indicated a chair at the table. "It's lunch time. Can you join me?" Pennelope wanted to know.

"If it isn't any trouble, then sure," Veronica agreed.

"Here, take Poppy," Pennelope said shifting the baby in her arms to Veronica. "I'll get it all out and we can visit. My, is this ever nice. I'm so glad you came over," Pennelope said as she started puttering around the little kitchen arranging dishes and silverware.

"I *chust* made a batch of Vernon Lonnie's Southern Gal Biscuits for them this morning. I'll be back in a second. There's a few left from breakfast," she said as she dashed next door to the big house.

The warm bundle in Veronica's arms took her breath away. She sat there staring at the tiny person with wonder. *I will never get to do this again,* she told herself. *A little living miracle. So special. Why not my very own? Why did she have to die?* Veronica took a deep breath then and the baby in her arms startled at the movement. *I wonder if a single person could adopt. Hm. An interesting thought. Maybe,* chust *maybe that would be a possibility.* Before the tears welling up in her eyes could fall, Pennelope rushed back into the little kitchen and spoke up, breaking the spell the little one had put Veronica into.

"I've been bringing in the garden here," Pennelope

continued talking as she gathered lunch together. "There's so much *kumming* now all at once I decided to make Ratatouille today."

"And what in the world is that?" Veronica chuckled.

"When I was little and we went camping one year, we were set up next to a family from Italy. It was one of those big campgrounds, *ya* know. The *mamm* spoke enough English, you see, but she only had two boys. I think she probably had always wanted a girl, too. I must have been around twelve. She invited me in one evening while she was cooking. She was making it for the family in a big cast-iron skillet. They'd brought along a whole bucket full of vegetables from her garden. She'd grown it all at home: onions, garlic, eggplant, zucchini, tomatoes, green beans, even fresh oregano. She sautéed the onion and garlic in olive oil first and then added all the rest, sort of cubed. My, that smelled wonderful! After the onions, garlic, eggplant, green beans and zucchini were pretty well cooked, she added the chopped tomatoes and the minced oregano, maybe a sprinkle of basil if you've got any, with some salt and pepper. We like it with some Parmesan cheese on it. It's been one of my favorites ever since. It's sort of a poor farmer's stew, she said, in the fall when the garden was petering out. They had it over rice or spaghetti, she told me. I sent it in to Maudie at *The Budget* not that long ago. It's such a yummy way to use up all the veggies that *kumm* all at once. She sat me down, back then, too, and gave me a bowl of it," she chuckled.

"I want to write that down," Veronica said, rummaging through her purse with one hand for a pen and the notebook she always carried there. "I love eggplant, but I never quite know all you can do with it. Have you ever tried Baba ganoush?"

"Baba-what? What kind of a name is that?" Pennelope demanded.

"I love this stuff," Veronica began. "A woman at the farmer's market had recipe cards she was giving out. It is Mediterranean, I think. I also once saw it in a Jewish Cookbook, too. I think the woman at the market was Romania. It's an eggplant dip made from roasted or grilled eggplant, tahini—I get it at the co-op, sesame butter, like peanut butter—olive oil, lemon juice, garlic, and salt. That's it. I like it best on sourdough *brode* for breakfast. I grilled it first in my little camping thing-y. I *chust* kept turning it till it was cooked and soft. Then when it is cool you peel it and mash it in with the rest. I should tell Maudie about this one, too *eh?*"

"Are you turning into a health food nut now?" Pennelope asked in jest.

"Actually, I think so. I think we eat far too much refined foods and processed stuff. It can't be *gut* for you. Look how big some people are getting. Then you hear more and more people are getting diabetes and high blood pressure. Instead of pills, I think diet is a huge factor," Veronica added, nodding. "Especially sugar and flour. Hardly the way I think we're meant to eat, not so much fresh anymore. My friend Ruth has completely cut off all sugar and flour of any kind and claims she's lost weight *chust* by doing that and feels a whole lot better too."

Veronica looked down at the baby in her arms. "Ooooh, look how sweet!" she said. "How she sticks her little tongue out!" Veronica bent down and kissed Poppy on the head.

Pennelope nodded in agreement. "Do you see anything else?"

"No, should I?" Veronica asked.

"Poppy has Downs," Pennelope said.

"No!" Veronica was shocked. "Really?"

"She's pretty healthy but she may need heart surgery soon. Other than that she's lucky there's nothing else going on. We've all fallen in love with her. She's as cute as button, eh?" Pennelope asked.

"Wow. Is that hereditary?" Veronica wanted to know. "The doctors told me that could be a possibility when everything was going wrong when I was carrying mine. They didn't say though after she was born. I don't really know what it was. Oh, you poor little darling."

"She's fine otherwise. She's actually quite precious. Her *mamm* and *dat* were upset at first. The doctors weren't all that encouraging about her prognosis—how she'll be, *ya* know, in the years to *kumm*. Downright pessimistic those doctors were. They didn't want them to get their hopes up, is how I figure. What her chances were like. They said only fifty-fifty percent she'd survive the delivery. Since then, her pediatrician has been really *gut*. He is so much more positive. Really optimistic. And they've gotten in touch with other families with special needs *kinner,*" Pennelope explained. "There's a little magazine called 'Life's Special Sunbeams' by other *Amische* parents with special *kinner,* that people write into."

"Do they blame themselves, maybe?" Veronica wanted to know. "Some do, *ya* know. They think they've sinned so this is their fault. *Gott's* punishment."

"Oh no. That's not true. Not at all," Pennelope insisted.

"I know that," Veronica agreed.

Pennelope continued. "But I don't think we can generalize here. Perhaps some consider that it is their fault, but many others feel honored that *Gott* chose their family especially for this particular child. I know these *kinner* bring much joy to all around them. Yes, it can be a monumental challenge—with a houseful of little ones and all the care they'll need, doctor trips, special diets, it can be a lot, I imagine totally overwhelming sometimes--but when a community pitches in, it is a huge blessing. Some say these children can see angels."

Veronica thought on that a while. "I wouldn't say I'd be disappointed or crushed if I had one. But my own baby had so much wrong, I still don't think I'd want to go through that again. But to *chust* have babies that you know have that possibility, no, actually that probability...I *chust* don't know."

"You should get some testing done and get some answers, *ya* know," Pennelope suggested. You need to know one way or the other, is my thinking."

"Oh, I am. This midwife, Ruth, is looking into a genetic specialist. I think I am ready to know what happened back then and what my chances are of it being passed down again."

"Here, I want you to read something that a *mamm* sent to Poppy's *mamm* who also has a child with Downs." Pennelope went into the hallway between her apartment and the main house and brought back a small wooden plaque.

"I'll read it to you," she said as she sat down. "This is the best!" Pennelope began reading.

Welcome To Holland
by Emily Perl Kingsley

I am often asked to describe the experience of raising a child with a disability—to try to help people who have not shared that unique experience to understand it, to imagine how it would feel. It's like this...

When you're going to have a baby, it's like planning a fabulous vacation trip—to Italy. You buy a bunch of guide-books and make your wonderful plans. The Coliseum. The Michelangelo David. The gondolas in Venice. You may learn some handy phrases in Italian. It's all very exciting.

After months of eager anticipation, the day finally

arrives. You pack your bags and off you go. Several hours later, the plane lands. The flight attendant comes in and says, "Welcome to Holland."

"Holland?!?" you say. "What do you mean Holland? I signed up for Italy! I'm supposed to be in Italy. All my life I've dreamed of going to Italy."

But there's been a change in the flight plan. They've landed in Holland and there you must stay.

The important thing is that they haven't taken you to a horrible, disgusting, filthy place, full of pestilence, famine, and disease. It's just a different place.

So, you must go out and buy new guidebooks. And you must learn a whole new language. And you will meet a whole new group of people you would never have met.

It's just a different place. It's slower paced than Italy, less flashy than Italy. But after you've been there for a while and you catch your breath, you look around...and you begin to notice that Holland has windmills...and Holland has tulips. Holland even has Rembrandts.

But everyone you know is busy coming and going from Italy...and they're all bragging about what a wonderful time they had there. And for the rest of your life, you will say "Yes, that's where I was supposed to go. That's what I had planned."

And the pain of that will never, ever, ever, ever go away...because the loss of that dream is a very, very significant loss.

But if you spend your life mourning the fact that you didn't get to Italy, you may never be free to enjoy the very special, the very lovely things...about Holland.

The two women were quiet then, each with her own thoughts. The only sound was Poppy softly cooing. Veronica looked down at the precious baby on her lap. A tear dropped onto the baby's face then, causing her to startle and blink her eyes several times before she laughed uproariously. A proper baby giggle.

"It's all such a mystery, *eh?*" Veronica wondered.

"It is. But I wouldn't trade this one for all the tea in China!" Pennelope declared.

They each reached for a handkerchief then and continued to take it all in.

"Back when I was teaching school, I found a book in the library. It hasn't occurred to me again in all this time till now. It made a deep impression on me. It was about a boy who was born completely helpless. This baby, Oliver, was born severely handicapped--blind, non-verbal, crippled, helpless. This is a true story, too. Word for word. Despite the doctors' bleak prognosis—they recommended just making him comfortable and not feeding him, letting nature take its course so to speak. Anyway, his dear parents took him home, where they and their children cared for him. He died when he was thirty-three years old."

Veronica continued. "Well, when Oliver's older brother was in his twenties and getting to know this girl, he brought her home. Before dinner, the brother invited the girl to go with him to Oliver's room to feed him his *mosch* for supper. The girl stood there and kind of *chust* cringed, not interested at all in the child. He eventually broke it off with that girl. Then when he was getting serious about another girl—I don't remember how many it was in the end—they all were really turned off by Oliver and the fact that the whole family felt so blessed to be able to care for him. Finally, one girl agreed to go in when the brother was going to feed Oliver--I think he was always fed from a red bowl if I remember correctly—this one girl asked at one point if she could have a turn feeding Oliver. That is when the older brother decided this girl was the one for him, that his little brother was able to choose for him. And they were married soon after."

"That is quite a story. Wow," Pennelope said, shaking her head.

CHAPTER 20
Fear of the Unknown

In fact, Ruth did know where to turn to figure out Veronica's dilFranny. She basically wanted to know if she would be able to have healthy children in the future or was that simply unrealistic? She was ready to hear either way and just get on with her life.

Ruth had come over to update Veronica on the moms that would be giving birth in the district in the next few weeks. They went over the charts while sharing a pot of coffee—complete with the rich camel milk, and fresh Aussie Bites.

"What are these things, Veronica? They are out of this world!" Ruth exclaimed, helping herself to a second tiny muffin.

"They're called Aussie Bites. I think they must have originated in Australia. Some of the bakeries have them but I have been experimenting and I think they came out pretty *gut*."

Ruth pressed on. "You have got to give me the recipe. Like today,"

she insisted.

"Sure," Veronica grabbed her recipe tin off the sideboard and began copying the recipe for her friend on an index card, reading it aloud as she wrote.

"1 cup oat flour and ¾ cup rolled oats
I have made it with an egg or two and it's less crumbly.
¼ cup dried apricots, prunes, figs or dates
¼ cup raisins or cranberries
¼ cup coconut sugar or brown/cane sugar...I've skipped the sugar because there's honey or maple syrup in it already.
¼ cup shredded coconut, unsweetened
¼ cup cooked, or raw quinoa
¼ cup sunflower seeds and/or pumpkin seeds
¼ cup flax meal
2 tablespoons chia seeds
1 teaspoon cinnamon
I've tried it with a pinch of ground cardamom. It is really *gut* that way.
¼ teaspoon pink or sea salt
¼ teaspoon baking soda
⅓ cup coconut, olive oil, or butter, melted
¼ cup maple syrup, honey, or agave nectar
½ teaspoon vanilla extract"

Veronica read on, "Preheat the oven to 350 degrees. Lightly grease a 24-count mini muffin pan.

1. Add all the oats, flour, and flaxseed, sunflower seeds, coconut, quinoa, chia seeds, and baking soda to the bowl. Stir well. Chop the apricots, raisins, and dates, prunes, figs and cranberries— whatever you like—into small bits. Put those in, too.

2. Pour in the honey, or maple syrup or agave, oil, and vanilla extract. Stir *chust* until combined.
3. Divide the batter among buttered or oiled muffin cups.
4. You can also let it sit in a cool place overnight so all the dry ingredients get softened.
5. Bake in a preheated oven for 10-12 minutes until golden brown.
6. Remove the pan from the oven and let cool in the pan on a cooling rack.

Once completely cooled, remove the muffins from the pan and store in an airtight container and refrigerate for a week or two."

And with that Veronica handed Ruth the recipe card. Then she forged ahead with what she had hoped Ruth could help her resolve. It had been festering in her mind ever since the birth of her premature baby seven years ago now. Veronica explained what she knew about her baby girl, which was, in fact, very little. Practically nothing. Huge advances were being made in the big city teaching hospitals in the Midwest, but none of that knowledge was being shared in the more remote rural parts of the states. It would take more years to trickle down to the tiny towns that served the Plain communities who had intentionally settled away from the cities. It was notoriously difficult to attract young doctors to move out to the country, though their training would have been a huge boon to the area. Some of the university hospitals were even advertising that they would pay off a doctor's student loans *and* depts in full in exchange for a two-year commitment to serve in these far-flung places; all the while studies and research continued to make advances, particularly in the areas of prematurity and genetics.

Veronica hesitated. "Did you think of anything, then?"

"We'll start off at the Fairview University Hospital of Minnesota," Ruth began. "By requesting your records from that time to be sent to them, they can begin to rule out what it might not be and make some guesses about what to check out next. They'll want you to come in next--we'll go together —and do all sorts of blood work. They can now test you for all sorts of inherited conditions that you could possibly pass on to your children. They should be able to give you a relatively concise picture from all that. There are huge grants that pay for this kind of work. Twenty years ago, this wouldn't have been possible. And in the end, they might be able to give you some answers. They might not, too, but we'll see what they say, okay?" Ruth concluded.

"Well, that is a relief, for sure," Veronica said after taking a deep breath. "I didn't know they might be able to figure any of it out." Veronica was absorbed in her thoughts for a moment. "*Denki,* Ruth. This means a lot, though if I am honest, I am afraid of what I might find out."

CHAPTER 21
Keepers of the Home

Veronica opened the umbrella and made a dash down the driveway to the mailbox. The ducks took this as an invitation to play and set up a huge din as they charged down the drive after her, always hopeful for a tasty handout. They were disappointed today. No such luck. They would have to seek out the slugs on their own. If they were extra lucky and it rained enough, plump night crawlers would emerge onto the grass in an hour or two to avoid being drowned down below in the mud. But today they didn't follow her back to the house. "I know, guys," she addressed the ducks. "No, I'm not bringing you food. Slugs, I mean. Better luck tomorrow, yous all." They faced her as she spoke. Not a peep. Dejected ducks. Oh well. They will forgive her another day when she coughed up the treats.

The mailbox was full. Taking out the pile, she carefully lifted up her old work apron and folded it over the bundle, holding it close to her chest to keep it all dry before running back to the kitchen. She left the umbrella open to dry in the mud room and wiped her bare feet on the rag rug just inside the kitchen door.

She separated out the junk mail first, dropping it in the kindling basket by the wood stove. Then after pouring a cup of coffee, she sat down to peruse the rest. And of course, right on schedule, there was a thick letter from Henry Eicher.

She had dreaded this one in particular. She had given him a final 'no' in her last letter. No, they were not meant for each other. No, she would not be marrying again. And no, no more *bobbeli* for her. Case closed. He couldn't argue any longer. Yes, she could agree they did have a lot in common, but then so would many other *Amische fraus* out there. In all of Canada, for Pete's sake.

Dear Veronica,

    Greetings of love in our dear Lord's Name!

    Thank you for your last letter. I know it wasn't an easy letter for you to write. You have been through an impossibly hard time and come through it all admirably. Your group of friends have helped I am sure, and I was particularly happy to hear how busy you are keeping. And now you'll be training as a midwife assistant to boot. Sorry, I am not poking fun. It doesn't really sound like your 'thing,' but stranger things have happened, eh?

Veronica lifted up the mug and took a gulp. "Like a buggy accident, you mean," she said aloud to no one in particular.

Well, now, this is the way I see things. Chust *hear me out. I figure we have four options here. Yes, both of us. First, you can call off all letters and that's it, and I'll respect that. Two, I could* kumm *down there and meet you and we can look at all the possibilities. And of course, continue to pray for direction. Three…you could take a little side trip and* kumm *up here. (It's only a little over eight-hundred miles away!) The Greyhound is pretty dependable. You could stay in the big* haus *with my* bruder's *family. I could show you the area and we could* chust *talk again about what we are both thinking.*

And finally, fourth option, we could take a break and let things cool off and rethink this in a month or two or more. Whatever you want to do is okay with me. You take your time. Stay busy and enjoy the garden, too. They say, 'take time to smell the flowers'.

Your friend,

Henry

All day long Veronica could not put the letter out of her mind. Finally, she decided to have her supper and spend the rest of the evening reading or writing in bed. She and Ruth had stopped at the library in town on their way back from visiting the birthing clinic where the nurse took all the blood samples the University hospital had requested and would ship them by courier in the morning for testing. They would have to wait a month, but then should start getting some results back.

Veronica was glad she was pursuing these questions. She'd wondered long enough and was optimistic they could give her some answers and she could put an end to the wondering. Then she could get on with her life, knowing one way or the other what her prospects in reality really were, and not just keep guessing and forever sitting on the fence. She was ready to face the truth and move on. Not knowing had plagued her long enough. It wasn't healthy to do that. It only prolonged her indecision about marriage and children. If only she could end this infernal not knowing. Yes, she realized she had waffled on this long enough. She didn't want to spend the rest of her life with these questions hanging over her head. *Back into Your hands,* Gott, she silently prayed. *Your will be done....*

Dear Kitty,

Our wedding was a festive affair, my! So many friends and relatives. A perfect fall day, not too cold. Lots of visiting. I thought it was the best day of my life for sure. I didn't have a clue, then, did I? No idea what would happen in chust *a few short years... months, truth be told.*

I got pregnant right away. I was so excited I thought I'd burst. Mamm *was* chust *as giddy as I was about it. Tamar, Felicity and Suzy had already had* bobbeli, *so it wasn't Mamm's first time being a* grossmammi, *but you'd think it was. Like she was the one expecting all over again. Amos and I lived less than a mile away from* Dat's *farm so we could visit back and forth whenever we wanted to, she and I.*

Mamm would make a big dinner every other Sunday. We only had church every other week. The off Sunday left everyone free to visit or relax at home. When we did have church, on those Sundays the service could last three hours and there would be a big noon meal before everyone had to travel home. We'd do our visiting at whosever farm church was being held for the 'on' days. Avram's, Rufus' and Tamar's families would all pack up and come for the afternoon, always leaving before dusk. Dat *never liked driving home after dusk, even with the slow-moving sign on the back of the buggy and the gas lamps hanging on the corners of the buggy roof. He never did trust cars after dusk. Shoo-ed them out of the house in time to get home before dark. Peeling off whomever was still glomming onto his leg or jumping onto their* doddy's *back. He loved it. Those* kinner *made him mighty happy. I* chust *feel bad that I never gave him a grandchild.*

My pregnancy was going chust *fine until the midwife wanted me to have an ultrasound. Mamm said she never believed in all the new* ferhoodled *tests and things they were offering* mamms *now.*

She said women have been having babies chust *fine without them since the beginning of time. Well, I let the midwife talk me into having* chust *the one x-ray. That's when it all started. First, they thought the baby was too small for my dates. Then they thought there was too much fluid. Then they wanted to do this test or that test.* Mamm *wasn't worried, though. I sure was. I was petrified.* Mamm chust *told me to trust, that* Gott *puts the babies in there and He'll make sure they come out* chust *fine. Except when I was nearing my seventh month, I started having contractions. I was put on bed rest then. I stayed put for weeks. Three to be exact, but it felt like months. Things slowed down then, but I still wasn't gaining weight like I should be. The midwife said I couldn't have a home-birth like we'd planned with things not quite right. So, I worried even more. Amos didn't have a clue what to think. He brought me flowers; he even came home from town one day with a huge box of Godiva chocolates and it wasn't anywhere near Christmas or my birthday yet. I could tell he was worried, too. I found him in the clothes closet one night when I got up. He was on his knees praying for us. Why couldn't my pregnancies be like* Mamm's? *Nothing stopped her. Herding the sheep when a storm was* kumming, *hauling bushels of vegetables in from the garden, or wringing out several loads of wash in a morning. She'd be up canning till midnight and then be up again to make first breakfast for* Dat *before he left for the barn, get his* kaffi *made and give him a bit of donut or something to hold him over till she'd made us all breakfast when the* kinner *were up. What was wrong with me?*

I think—no, I know—Amish girls are automatically set up to become 'keepers of the home.' There are no blurry lines here as far as gender or our roles. We are either girls or boys. I cannot believe all the fuss over gender these days. Where did all that kumm *from, anyway? Well, boys are farmers or blacksmiths or saddle makers or have some equally masculine occupation. Girls are constantly exhorted to learn to sew—I started at three years old, for heaven's sake—to cook, bake, and learn all the homemaking skills that will be required when you marry. There is no room for any other aspira-tions. Well, maybe* chust *becoming an old maid schoolteacher. You grow up watching your older sisters and aunties filling up their cedar chests with all sorts of handmade items to be saved for that great day when you marry and have your own home. It has been this way since time immemorial. The roles are cast in stone, which is how pretty much all cultures work, I think, or I am guessing. Until someone rocks the boat. I'm not about to do that. Maybe in my next life. Now I do sound like a heretic. Oh dear. But there's that* Amische *nurse, Phoebe Schwartz, over in some settlement, who got to go to school to become a nurse. That was sure a surprise, progressive if you ask me. But sure helpful, too. I can't imagine.*

But now I am older and wiser, I think. I've seen everything that could go wrong, go wrong. Accidents, illness, addictions, deaths, all the things that make up this world. Many find forgiveness and some even find a deeper faith and gratitude for what they have, even through such sad events. Others dwell on their loss and struggle for years never finding meaning in such uninvited burdens. It makes a body wonder. In any adversity, why do some people thrive while others despair under the same circumstances? Is there something in their makeup or DNA that gives some folks seemingly supernatural strength while others are sorely lacking the resources to move ahead? Do those that not only survive but actually thrive pray more? Pray harder? Fast more? Do they know some secret that the rest of us aren't yet privy to? Well, I sure wish someone would clue me in then.

Does Gott *punish those that have sinned by striking them with untold tragedies that arise from apparently unexpected sources? Or is it all* chust *terribly random with no rhyme or reason? Have these horrible events been pre-destined, and we are required to simply accept and not question the reasons why? Is it even possible to numb one's mind and heart and not offend the Author of all Life by doubting His plans for us? As humans, are we even capable of such Herculean resignation?*

Am I strong enough? Absolutely not. But—and this is a big BUT—"I can do all things through Christ which strengtheneth me." - Philippians 4:13. I wish I could believe that.

I think back to when we were all little. There were seven of us under eight years old. The babies came every two years. Twins twice. I never really wondered where they came from. Maybe they were picked out at the hospital, like a grocery store and you went there to get them. There was always such excitement when we'd wake up to find one of the grossmammis *making our breakfast and our parents gone, and she'd tell us that they went to get the baby. Her excitement was contagious. When the van driver brought them back home, we'd hardly be able to contain ourselves, all pushing and shoving to get the first look. Mamm would settle on the sofa in the great room and we'd all huddle around trying to get a peek. We'd all reconvene later upstairs,* chust us kinner *to discuss the new arrival. The boys thought new babies looked too scrunched up or red. Mostly us girls were on cloud nine, hoping for a turn to hold it.*

A new day. I am hoping today is better, Veronica thought to herself. *Are there no silver linings for me? I don't know how I can bear much more. I decided to try to get out more. Show up for all the frolics when the* fraus *get together to quilt or bake or do the canning. It is nice to see everyone and get to know anyone new who has moved into the district, but then I can't stand it when people feel sorry for me and try to talk about the past or feed me all those horrible clichés: "You never know, you could marry again, Veronica." Or "You* chust *have to get out more and you'll meet someone Veronica... you could even have more* kinner, *you are young enough..." Those stupid sayings aren't worth the cost of the embroidery floss to sew them on a pillow. Spare me. That's the hardest. And when they are all passing around babies, all plump and happy.*

I can't even hold them anymore. I can hardly be glad for those mamms, *though I really am. Such little miracles. Why couldn't mine have been plump and happy? Why is it so unfair? Ach! Here I go again, and I haven't even fixed breakfast. Lord help me. Please. Show me... I'm afraid I've lost my way. I can't imagine this is how You would have me live always. Please, dearest Jesus.*

Some days are so gut *and then these others...*

Veronica got up and finished dressing, hoping to somehow shake her unhappy mood. She brushed her hairs in the mirror, twisting it all into a tight bun and clipped her *kapp* in place. Just before she left the room, she turned back to the dresser top where her little inspirational calendar sat. *So, Catherine. Do you have any wisdom for me today?* she asked herself. She paged through it until she found today's date and read:

"As you grow in love, you help each other, gently, peacefully, constantly, accepting the weaknesses of each other with deep love and great patience, for that is how the Lord has treated you. Your goal is to become a family, a 'community of love,' accepting all the pain, the problems, the difficulties that every family must go through if it is going to become a community of love."

Curious, she thought to herself. *Food for thought for sure.* She continued thinking about it as she descended the stairs into the kitchen. *Like that one today... it was* chust *meant for me. Humph.*

CHAPTER 22

Auction Day

Auction day came only once a year in the district where Veronica lived. It was a time-honored institution, which began in order to raise money for the one-room schoolhouse. The Amish pay taxes on their land, along with any other taxes their respective counties charge, but the little private schools are on their own there. The families are depended upon not only to see to the upkeep of the building, inside and out, but there are also all the supplies, the teacher's salary, textbooks, and all the other teaching aids and equipment.

Families frequently kept the auction in mind when they moved or downsized a home, setting aside items no longer needed. Some *dats* and their sons used the extra time during the winter to carve toys and farm animals and construct little toy barns to add to the donations at the auction. There is always no shortage of quilts and other homemade items. Sometimes two school districts will agree to combine their efforts and hold a joint event. Huge tents are rented to house each category of contributions: furniture in one tent, farm implements in another; garden plants and even small trees and bushes are often on offer. Then quilts and crafts in another. Each tent has its own *Amische* auctioneer. Hundreds of folding chairs and benches will be set up ahead of time in each tent. Not only *Amische* attend schoolhouse auctions, but lots of *Englischers;* many are tourists who just happen to be passing through, others from the surrounding area often also show up, mostly out of curiosity and a chance to rub shoulders with 'real' Amish people. (I never heard of 'unreal' Amish folks. Have you?) You can easily tell the difference between the two by their dress alone. Then there are the sheer numbers, *Amische* far outnumbering their *Englische* neighbors.

There is always a food tent, too. Everyone brings some bakery item to share or a local *Amische* bakery will cater the event. An auction can go on all day. You could get mighty hungry or thirsty sitting there while the callers drone on and on, and dressers and rockers and tables and chairs are hauled up to the front and then hauled down to the back as they are bought and sold. Donuts are the standard fare for these affairs. It is a great way to catch up with friends and meet your neighbors. There are always other tables set up where canned goods are sold: jams, jellies, apple butter, sauerkraut, chow-chow, and pickles can be bought, the proceeds all going into the school fund.

There is always the designated parking lot for all the buggies and cars, too. A separate site for parking bicycles is also cordoned off. Barefoot children run between the tents enjoying the excitement while toddlers watch all the goings on from their perches high up on their *dats* shoulders. It is always fun to meet friends and catch up on any news. Today was no different. Veronica didn't plan on bidding on anything, but always liked to see what was on offer anyway, and it was always great fun to bump into old friends, too.

"Why, Veronica, I haven't seen you in a coon's age!" Clara

Miller gushed as she came up to Veronica and greeted her. "How are you? I was *chust* thinking about you the other day. So where have you been keeping yourself?"

"I'm fine. Keeping busy, the usual," Veronica replied cooly. "How are you?" she added quickly deflecting the focus from herself. She knew Clara would be fishing for any gossip today especially.

"Well, our oldest, Suzy got married and Jonathan is getting married this November," Clara was eager to share with her. "The others are still home except Fern is off helping her *mammi* and *doddy* pack up and move to my brother Ray's soon. They *chust* built the *dawdi haus* there for them. Rebecca is still living at home but teaching in our school. It's her second year."

Veronica liked Clara well enough, but she was wary at the same time. She knew her to be inquisitive by nature, but she could be downright nosy when she wanted to be. Well, there it was, not surprising Veronica in the least.

"I was *chust* wondering," Clara rattled on. "Have, um, are you getting to know any, you know, well, prospective husbands? I think about you all the time, keeping that in my prayers, *ya* know. It's been more than enough time. Any nibbles in that department? Cause if there aren't, have I got someone for you. He—"

Veronica needed to put a stop to this conversation, now, before it went any further, and butted right in. "Actually, I have decided not to get to know anyone...in that way. I am quite content how I am now. Please don't worry yourself. It's a closed subject Clara." Her glare directed right at the woman stopped her. The message could not have been more clear.

Clara immediately took offense, taking this personally. Wasn't she just trying to help? Show love and concern? She stammered, "Well, you sound sure. You, you could be more open, *ya* know, let friends help *ya*...."

Veronica concluded the exchange by walking away, thinking a coffee at this point sounded like just the ticket. Clara was left standing there with her mouth open, just as one of her grandchildren came up to her. "Can we get donuts *Mammi?* Please? Huh? Please?"

The day became hotter by noon. Toddlers were whining, having missed their naps, and families were settling themselves on blankets laid out under trees scattered over the property, opening picnic baskets. The Amish auction callers continued to push the items that continued to be brought up to the front in each of the three big tents. Boys brought water to the horses while small children continued to run riot, now each holding a giant iced donut topped with colored sprinkles.

Veronica sipped her coffee while perusing the tables set up in the food tent for the smaller vendors there today. One table was selling homemade plush ponies and lambs. Another was piled high with new Tupperware, its *Amische mamm* pointing out further items in the catalogues there. Another table was displaying essential oils, handmade soaps and scented candles, embroidered tea towels, quilted hot pads and numerous other handmade craft items. Many of the women throughout the Amish world have taken it upon themselves in recent years to start up small businesses to bring in a little extra income at home, proving themselves to be quite inventive, if not creative.

CHAPTER 23

Summer in a Jar

Dearest Kitty,

A new day. Do you think I'll ever get published? Pride. That's all this is. Ambition. Is that really a sin?

"Scratch that," she told herself out loud before continuing.

Mamm had it all figured out: what day to bake brode *for the week. What day to do the washing. What day to make pies, what day to clean the house. That was always on Saturdays. Sundays we weren't allowed to do much of anything except church or visiting and eating, taking walks, and reading. Napping.*

V eronica stopped writing and got up from the kitchen chair, reminded of the little nuggets of wisdom hanging on the opposite wall. Walking over to the wall by the pantry off the kitchen she found what she was looking for. It had been a wedding gift all those years ago. Its wisdom was just as fresh today, however. Its author would remain anonymous forever, in the spirit of *Amische* humility.

Eight laminated cards were carefully spaced out along a

brown grosgrain ribbon that was hanging from a nail in the wall. Each card contained a prayer that had been exquisitely lettered by hand and embellished with doves and flowers. It wouldn't hurt to reflect on these little meditations often.

Monday—Wash Day

Help me God, to wash
away all my selfishness
and vanity, that I may
serve You with perfect
humility through
the week ahead.

"That's a *gut* one," she told herself out loud, nodding in agreement with that thought. Then she continued reading.

Tuesday—Ironing Day

Lord, help me to iron
out all the wrinkles of
prejudice I have accumulated
through the year so that I
may see Beauty in
others.

Wednesday—Mending Day

Oh God, help me to mend
my ways so that I will
not set a bad example
for others.

Thursday—Cleaning Day

Lord Jesus, help me to
reach the dust of all the
many faults I have been
hiding in the secret
corners of my heart
all these years.

Veronica turned back toward the table and picked up her coffee mug to refill it at the stove before returning to the prayers on the wall. *Such* gut *reminders,* she told herself as she sipped the piping hot drink.

Friday—Shopping Day

Oh God, give me the grace to
be a wise and prudent shopper so
that I may purchase eternal
happiness for myself and
my family and all in
need of my love.

Saturday—Cooking Day

Help me, my Savior, to
brew up a large kettle of
brotherly love and serve it
with the clean sweet

bread of human kindness.

Sunday—The Lord's Day

Oh God, since I have now
prepared my house for You
please come into my heart as
my honored Guest so that I
may spend the day in
Your presence.
- Amen

The hanging chain of prayers concluded with one last
thought:

This is the day which
the Lord hath made; we will
rejoice and be glad in it.
Psalm 118:24

Refreshed, she returned to the table again and began writing.

When we were little, we loved brode *day. The younger ones were happy crawling around the floor or playing with their toys while* Mamm *kneaded the dough. She'd break off small chunks for us four older ones to knead along with her. We'd punch them, roll them, fold them and punch them again,* chust *like how we thought* Mamm *was doing it. Those little lumps would fall on the floor, or we'd take nibbles off of them, or lick them, and finally* Mamm *would carefully pick off any dust or cat hairs and line them all up on a greased tray and cover them with a towel to rise next to her big proving bowls containing her dough balls growing up and over the rims all on their own. We insisted that they be lined up according to our ages so we could claim ours when they came out of the oven, and not get mixed up, as if our own would look or taste any different from any of the others. Then we'd bound off to play or go to the barn and visit with* Dat. *She would prepare dinner while all that* brode *doubled in size. Once they came out of the oven, we'd all clammer to cradle our hot little loaves in our hands and spread them thick with jam for a midmorning snack. Nothing ever tasted so good as those funny-looking, misshapen little blobs of* brode.

I often stayed behind to help cook. I took my training very seriously. I would be a wunderbar *cook, learning all there was to know about making pies, cakes, soups, roasts—all of it. My future family would devour my cooking while at the same time my heart*

would swell with love for all of them. Now, did that ever happen?
Nope....

Veronica took a deep breath and sighed then, thinking again of all she would not have in all the many years to come. She grabbed her coffee mug and took a huge gulp in the hope of washing away the feelings of longing that never seemed very far below the surface of her mind and heart. Then hurrying on she wrote once again.

Saturdays were usually baking day. Even without electricity she'd
manage to crank out half a dozen pies, a few cakes and all the
brode our family would need for the week. But before we started
any baking however, we needed to consult The Box—the all-impor-
tant tin box containing the recipes. If they passed the taste test and
the family, particularly Dat, *approved of it, the card would be filed*
in The Box, and not a minute before.

Now you have to understand my mamm. *She almost*
worshipped Maudie. Maudie has been writing for The Budget
since February, 1982. She has the cooking column in The Budget
and has become somewhat of what we now call a cult... at least a
following. Mamm *would carefully cut out Maudie's page when*
Dat *was done with the paper and read it over before trimming it*
and pasting it onto an index card. Then she'd put it in 'Purgatory,'
as she called it, that 'no-man's-land' where it sat in the blue-striped
crock on the shelf until she tried it out on us guinea pigs. We'd rate
the dish from a one to a ten. Tens and elevens made it into the recipe
box, no questions asked. Happy guinea pigs. The others would be
sent back to the crock to be considered again later unless they were a
three or less. Those went into the kindling box with the empty
cereal boxes and cardboard egg cartons. She has been cutting out
those recipes since the beginning. The little sketch of Maudie in The
Budget *depicts a plump, dimpled* mammi *now, though in the '80s*
she looked much younger, the sketch, that is. Sort of like Betty

Crocker. I read that she was never a real person, though her pictures on the covers of the cookbooks also aged over the years, chust *like Maudie's.*

A spiral bound cookbook was published with all of Maudie's recipes from the beginning until 1991. It was in its sixth printing that year. A more recent edition is now in the works being published by The Budget. *We are all waiting with bated breath. They are saying it will contain healthier options, reflecting much of the shift toward better eating and diet. Maybe not so many offerings calling for canned soup or jello or as much sugar and such. I am sure curious. Wonder if they'll tell you how to cook quinoa, or make lentil pilaf, though I've got that in my* Diet For a Small Planet. *Maudie's book is supposed to come out eventually. I've already been waiting for four years for it to appear.*

I loved Fridays. By six o'clock in the morning Mamm'd *have the kitchen humming while the rest of us all slept.* Dat *was usually up though, off to his barn chores. He'd have 'first breakfast' and then hightail it to check on the sheep. First breakfast was a cup of strong* kaffi *loaded with cream and sugar,* chust *to get you going. Maybe he'd grab a donut, that is if there was any to be found, being pretty rare with so many hungry* kinner *about. During the busiest part of lambing season, he'd sometimes sleep in the barn, throwing an old sleeping bag on a mound of hay. You don't want to miss a ewe having trouble. You could lose both of them, and they don't come cheap.*

'Second breakfast' was when everyone was up and could all meet at the table before work and school. It was a proper stick-to-your-ribs meal. If it was a Saturday when Mamm was baking, or canning, or a Monday when she did all the washing starting early, second breakfast would be something simple, like the oatmeal smorgasbord that you fixed yourself, all the options lined up on the table by the big pot of steaming oatmeal: walnuts, homemade granola which added chust *the right amount of crunch, sunflower seeds, honey, brown sugar, a pitcher of cream, raisins, dried cranberries,*

peanuts, shaved coconut, chocolate chips—each one of us had our favorites. Or corn meal mosch, made ahead and cooled and then cut into slabs and fried in butter or bacon grease. You'd pour on the maple syrup and cream. Sometimes it had scrapple in it, too. Our big meal was always at noon.

I'd feel so grownup, Mamm having me help her cook or can. She'd made me a grown-up apron years before I was old enough to have one, chust like hers in charcoal gray, chust for when it was the two of us cooking. I knew it wasn't chust busy work—to keep me out of her way. I really did pack the jars with hundreds of little cucumbers right out of the washing tub, first putting a clean grape leaf into the jar and then standing up all the pickles. The grape leaf keeps the pickles crisp. You didn't need alum then. Next the dill flowers went on top of that first layer, one sprig each, and then the next layer of pickles. When they reached the shoulder of the jars, you'd add a heaping tablespoon of pickling spice—chust one, and a peeled clove or two of garlic. Then I would hold the funnel and she'd carefully pour the hot brine over it all. I'd wipe all the rims off with a clean rag and lay the lids on. Then the rings would get twisted on real tight and they'd be ready for the canner. I could do it in my sleep now. She and I would be so happy, though we weren't supposed to become brot of it, but you couldn't help it looking at all those rows of perfect jars all cooling on the table. The best part was lying in bed when you'd cleaned up the whole kitchen, making it ready for the next day, being all worn out, listening to the lids pinging, one at a time: ping...ping...ping-ping-ping...ping...every night during canning season till the garden was picked clean, and we'd take Dat down to the root cellar to admire all the jars glistening with that year's bounty. "Summer in a jar" she called it. The colors were magnificent: shades of green of the different pickles, green beans, olive-colored tomatillo salsa, orange peach halves, red stewed tomatoes, ketchup, sauces, pink applesauce, yellow succotash, purple beets—one could get pretty brot of it all, though we shouldn't be— proud. I am chust laughing now at what he said that one year, *that maybe he could* chust *buy* Mamm *some colored sand to fill up the jars and save her all that work! He was like that. Clever.*

These days I daydream a lot and often think on the best times we had growing up. One time Dat *brought us all to the Hay River for the day. It was so hot even* Mamm *didn't want to stay home. We brought inner tubes and a huge picnic and jugs of cider up from the root cellar.* Mamm *couldn't get us to come out of the water even for lunch. She said we'd turn into prunes for sure, but we didn't believe her. (And I can't tell if we did.) That's the time I thought we'd lost Zorah for sure. She was on top of the smallest inner tube, and all of a sudden, the current pulled her away from the bend in the river where we were all playing, and she sped away from us downstream. We all started screaming at once and* Dat *jumped up with his shoes still on and ran down the bank and jumped in when he came up alongside her. I didn't think he knew how to swim but he caught her by the ankle and pulled her back to the bank.* Mamm *got us all to* kumm *out then and told us exactly how far we could play after that. We had to stay in the shallow part by our blanket.*

Another time when Rufus was about four and we were stuck inside during a thunderstorm, he pulled a pillowcase over his head and marched around on the big bed in our parents' room singing some silly nursery rhyme until he marched right off the end of the bed. The next minute us kinner *saw blood dripping down the pillowcase and he was still wiggling on the floor trying to get up and we all started screaming for* Mamm. *She came running up the stairs and got a gut look at him. He'd mashed his front teeth in such a way that they were all pushed back in the roof of his mouth.*

She called Dat *in from the barn, hitched up the buggy herself, packed Rufus up and took him into town to the dentist there, though she'd never been to see this one. Rufus told us later that the dentist was an older man who sprayed something into his face and then with his huge bare hands pulled the teeth back into place. They stayed there, too. He'd fixed it. It worked, which Mamm couldn't stop telling people about. The stuff he sprayed at Rufus was ether which sort of made him goofy for a bit, but he didn't cry when the teeth were forced back where they belonged. He spent most of supper that night—he could only eat ice cream or Jello for a couple of days—telling us about all the wild animal heads mounted around all the rooms at the dentist's. It turned out the guy was a big game hunter and went on safaris to Africa for his vacations and came back with all these exotic trophies. Mamm said it was enough to distract anyone from what was going on in the dentist's chair. His methods might have been a bit antiquated—from the Middle Ages more likely—but he sure knew his stuff. This was back in the 1980s. I don't know if people are still shooting endangered animals with guns. Only cameras now from what I've read.*

Once Dat brought home a big box from town and called us all outside. We could hear whimpering and scratching inside, and we all tried to guess what it could be. One said a turtle, and another thought a cat. It turned out to be this little puppy, so small it was surprising it had already been weaned. It was black and white. Dat told us it was a Border Collie. It would be up to us to name him. He was supposed to grow up knowing how to herd the sheep out in the paddocks. I couldn't figure out how he'd know without watching his mamm dog or his dat dog to learn how, but Dat said they chust knew. Dat got a bunch of books from the library on shepherding dogs and would tell us all these amazing stories about them at supper every night. He became quite the expert on them.

He explained how you work with your dog and teach him whistle commands telling him what you want him to do. Most of the books were from a bunch of orthodox monks—men living at a monastery place they call, New Skete in New York. He ordered a funny whistle from a catalogue; it was a triangle with three sides and each kind of sound means something else, like 'lie down' or 'come' or 'away' and they'll go out to the herd and do chust what you tell them to do. They can learn all this before they're a year old. We all tried teaching him until Dat said only he could give it orders or he'd get completely confused and not obey anyone in the end. We could watch Dat working with him for hours. We'd all sit on the top of the fence by the gate to the paddock, watching him teaching that little dog. Then one day Dat brought a sheep out with him and tried out the whistles on the dog and would you believe that dog knew exactly what to do?

His name was another matter altogether. We spent whole supper times making suggestions that no one liked or one we all hated. We called him "the puppy" for almost two weeks. Some of the rejects included Pup Tart, White Fang, and Lassie—from two of our school readers—and Little Bow Wow, and Blackjack.

Zorah came up with his name finally. She was sitting in the yard with him one day, by the flower bed. He loved nipping at them —the flowers--and would even eat some of them. She called him in later when she was going in the house, saying 'come on Ferdinand' and that little dog followed her. That was her favorite name from a book she'd often pick at bedtime about a big black Angus bull that liked to sit in the flowers in the fields.

Part Three

"Be slow to anger and quick to forgive, and you will have friends for as long as you live."

— AMISH PROVERB

CHAPTER 24
A Birth!

Dear Kitty,

You aren't going to believe this. I chust *have to tell someone.*

So, Ruth pages me at midnight. I don't know how to even answer this thing. We didn't practice. So, I push some buttons and yell hello into it, and I still can't hear her. So she texts and I read: "Get ready. Picking you up soon."

I run around like a chicken without a head, check the wood stove, shut down the damper, get dressed in the clean outfit I've had ready these past weeks, and close up the house. I wait for her on the porch. Sure enough a van drives up five minutes later and I hop in. Ruth tells me all about Mavis. Fifth baby. Very organized. Probably has Edward already arranging someone to take care of the cows, got the other kinner *sorted at some* grossmammi's.

Ruth tells me she apprenticed at Mavis's other kinners' *deliveries, too, under one of the clinic midwives. All easy births with the others, and in great health throughout this pregnancy also. She's carried the baby to term, which I guess means it's not early or premature; he or she has been growing nicely, not* kumming *too soon, not like mine...*Veronica took a deep breath then, the emotions surrounding her little baby bubbling up once again. *Marta is what I named her. Why couldn't she* chust *go along with the program and grow normally back then, is what I* wRuth *know.* She let out a long breath and composed herself. *Ok, but back to the story here,* she told herself and began to write again. *Ruth reports that Mavis took good care of herself, understands good nutrition, doesn't keep a lot of junk food around, keeps her house clean and tidy—one of the things she explains to me that she observes closely when considering a family's suitability for a home birth—and was excited that they had been blessed with yet another baby, though they didn't know if it was another little 'dish washer' or 'wood chopper' yet.*

*When we got there Mavis had everything all arranged: the farm and kids were all taken care of, she had done up the dirty dishes, the bed was made with a plastic sheet under fresh linens, with another full set under that for after the birth, and she was walking around the house in her homemade nightie and little hand knit slippers, grinning from ear to ear and blowing little puffs of air along with the contractions while Edward was nervously trying to work on a jigsaw puzzle she had obviously assigned to him (*chust *to keep him busy and occupied, I suspect.) She walked around for a while, sipping juice and taking short trips to the outhouse every hour or so. The bedroom had a freshly painted commode by the bed so she wouldn't have to leave the bedroom after the birth for the prescribed ten days. A nightstand was set up with everything she would need to care for the baby and herself right there: diapers, a diaper pail, baby clothes, her personal items, and an oil lamp.*

Ruth suggested I make a pot of coffee and make myself useful somehow, though I didn't see anything out of order that I could busy myself with. So, I stood by the stove and then served Ruth and Edward some coffee.

Things slowed down around four in the morning. Ruth suggested Mavis use the time to nap, but Mavis was all business and suggested using 'the combs.' I had never heard of this, neither had

Ruth, so she showed us the pressure points along the base of your thumbs which can be stimulated to help with contractions. She made two fists around two small hair combs and, sure enough, got the contractions going again in no time. About an hour later she made a bee-line for the bedroom, had Edward light a kerosene lamp and hold it up for Ruth, propped herself up on the bed, though I expected if she was close she'd be huffing and puffing, maybe groaning. I didn't know what to expect, but I think Ruth also thought it couldn't quite be time, that things could not have picked up that fast, but after a couple more rather sedate, lady-like puffs, she started pushing. Before I could grab the towels on the dresser to have ready for Ruth, out barreled an eight and a half-pound wood chopper and promptly howled his arrival! It was more like his adamant disagreement with the state he now found himself in. It for sure wasn't the cozy nest he'd been in for nine months! Leave it to efficient Mavis. We should have been more prepared. They hadn't really needed us at all, Ruth told me later. They knew exactly how to do this. It was utterly amazing. I don't have words for it.

Edward then picked up and held his baby while Ruth delivered the placenta into a large stainless-steel bowl, which they would bury under the eaves of the house, an old Amish tradition. Then Ed spoke for the first time all night: he told us how with their first baby he had been so afraid of poking him with a pin while diapering him that when he finally finished and tried to pick up the baby, found him stuck to the bed—he had pinned the diaper to the sheets! We sure laughed then, me still so blown away and nervous but Ruth was as cool as a cucumber.

Then Edward looked down at Mavis and says, "Well, Maw, what should we name him?"

And she says, "Oh, Paw, I dunno. What do you wRuth name him?"

"Well, I dunno," he says. After five kids, surely they knew how to do this, I think to myself. After a minute or so he added, "Maybe

we should get the hat." Then he saunters off, baby still tucked into his arm.

So he got his black Sunday hat from its peg high up in the kitchen by the wood stove and lays it on the bed. Then he settled the baby back on the bed next to Mavis and cut up little pieces of paper and they both wrote down their favorite boy names and folded them up and dropped them in the hat. I still didn't know where this was going. Then he picked up the baby and gently put the baby's hand into the hat, all the while Ruth running after him and switching out another warm blanket over the bobbel. When he did that, the baby's hand opened up as his arm was extended and then shut into a fist when it touched the bottom of the hat. He was supposed to pick his own name!

His father pried the scrap of paper out of the tiny fist and opened it. A huge smile spread across his face. He looked up at me and asked,

"You ready?" I nodded.

Then he announced, "His name is Elmer!" They both positively beamed at each other then, a long, loving look into each other's eyes. So that was how they did it. He could never blame them for some name he didn't like. He had chosen it himself.

Grandma Lizzie and another grossmammi showed up soon after that. The sun was already peeking up then after Elmer arrived and the mammis made us all a wonderful breakfast of steaming oatmeal topped with fresh cream and homemade granola on top of that and coffee. I am thinking, someday, perhaps thirty or forty years from now I will think back to my first birth. Not my own, but as a midwifery apprentice. By then I am sure Elmer will have a house full of his very own little wood choppers and dish washers.

CHAPTER 25

Bucket Lists

After the birth Veronica invited Ruth in for coffee. Ruth went over the details of the labor and birth, and further explained what they had seen. Veronica could happily do without the technical parts of it. It was just so wonderful. It was perfect. Their prayers had been answered and Mavis's *bobbel* had arrived safely.

Settled at the table for coffee, too wound up still to think about catching up on their sleep, they shared a pot of decaf and a plate of Bachelor Button cookies.

Veronica slowly sipped her coffee while thinking how to broach her question. She had been mulling over this one for a while.

"Ruth, how is it that you never married? Did you go courting at all?" she asked rather delicately. Ruth was a very comely woman with a warm, kind manner.

"Oh, yes. I did—court. For about six months. It was over ten years ago now. Ivan was very sweet. His family had *kumm* from out of state and moved here. We kept it all hush-hush, thinking we'd wait to let everyone know closer to when they'd read the banns at church. It didn't dawn on us that it was any more than a coincidence that we both had the same last name. We kind of kidded about that back then. Lapp is certainly a common enough name, going back to the beginning for sure. Then one night he came over to formally meet my parents and ask for their blessing. They were delighted and made a big fuss, their first daughter getting married. We visited for quite a while and then my *dat* asked about his parents and grandparents. Before long, he asked Ivan to name all his uncles. *Dat* went and got a yellow notepad from his rolltop oak desk and had Ivan list all of them and the names of their *fraus*, too. *Dat* looked at it a long while, stroking his beard and frowning, and then showed the pad to *Mamm*. Turned out we were second cousins. Everyone had forgotten to check that since the rest of his family were still all out east."

Veronica shook her head. "That's terrible! I would die!"

"Well, I couldn't die, but boy, were we rattled. We went to the bishop, and he looked at the family tree we had drawn up and he *chust* said it was clear. We couldn't marry. I must have cried for a whole month afterwards. I bet Ivan did too. We parted, so sorry for not thinking to check in the beginning. He eventually moved back east. I know of another girl that happened to, too. It actually made her sick. She pined away for months and finally had to get some medication to settle her nerves. She still isn't all there even after all this time. It was such a pity. At least I could come through it and not *chust* give up on living like she did. But I was never asked to court again after that. It *chust* didn't happen. I had hoped it might. I guess in the back of my mind I'd still be open to it, though I am getting on in years now."

"Is it really a bad idea to marry second cousins? I mean, what could happen? Who made the laws concerning it anyway?" Veronica wanted to know.

"Well," Ruth began. "I read that no matter how related

two family members are, they all share some genes in common. Which means they are also more likely to share any gene versions that can lead to disabilities. This is why close family members are more likely to have a child with disabilities. They are more likely to share the same 'problem' genes and so more likely to each pass them down to their children, too."

She continued, "So when our church elders learned this a generation ago or more maybe, it made sense to issue some suggestions or recommendations and discourage close relatives marrying. Some churches or districts are stricter than others. Some are very legalistic, with a right to be, they believe. Others are more lenient. Others simply threw out the science and counselled their congregations to trust the Lord and not worry about such things. Some ignored the occasional consequences, which they tended to discredit, saying it would have happened anyway, could have happened to anyone. No one knows for sure which way is right. It's certainly not cut and dry."

Ruth paused, and then continued. "Some families feel shame that they have a child with a disability or syndrome or something. I personally don't think that is the universal experience, though. And I don't think anyone, bishops or ministers or anyone else would lay that on a family, you know, like they sinned, and *Gott* is cursing them or something. I sure hope not. I don't think it is the stigma that it is in some cultures, though you read about families that keep a child or a relative out of sight, or even give them up to an institution for the feeble-minded. I wonder if that is even done anymore. Yikes, pretty backward, I would think."

That got Veronica thinking. "I've also heard about families with a child with Down Syndrome who felt they had been singularly blessed, that these special children were chosen for their family especially by *Gott*. That they are the happiest little souls on earth, and they bring something to each family they are born into. It makes me wonder. But I still don't know if I would set out to have them, if my genes are bad or something."

That left them both with lots to ponder. Finally, Veronica spoke up.

"Maybe you can have my Canadian suitor. That would be *wunderbar,* Ruth. I for sure don't want him," Veronica added chuckling. "Why, that would solve everything."

Horrified at the thought, Ruth shot right back, "But I couldn't take him from you. Never!"

"Not even if I still don't want him?" Veronica asked slyly, titling her head.

"Let's *chust* see what the genetic tests say about you first, okay?" Ruth concluded.

Ruth went on, chuckling. "Did I tell you what my Aunt Agnes did one year?"

Veronica shook her head. "Well," Ruth continued. "Have you ever heard of 'speed dating?" Veronica shook her head again.

"Well, there's a really sweet waitress at the coffee shop in town and she took her break and joined Aunt Agnes last time she went there after shopping. She wanted to tell my aunt she was dating someone. He was a nice, Christian man she'd met at this restaurant that had set up this event for single people in the area. She said there were about forty people there that night. She'd never tried it before. How it works is that there is a man at each of the ten tables and a woman rings a bell, and all the women line up and the first group sit at each the table and they talk for six minutes and then when the bell rings again they move to the next fella, and so on until all of the women have met all of the men. Each guy has a piece of paper, and he makes notes by the names of the women he might be interested in knowing, and all of the women write down their preferences and if any match, the moderator will call them later and set up a date. That's how they met! I'd never heard of anything so *ferhoodled* in my life! Anyway, Aunt Agnes goes and signs me up for the next speed dating night! Have you ever? I mean, really? As if I'd ever even consider marrying an *Englischer!*"

"Did you go?" Veronica wanted to know, horrified at the prospect.

"Of course, I didn't go. You think I could have? Never in a million years," Ruth flatly stated, her voice inching up by decibels. "And there have been others playing matchmaker for me over the years. I'm *chust* not interested. It isn't a big deal. I actually think Auntie is losing a few marbles. She's getting a bit senile if you ask me."

The next morning dawned bright and balmy. Perfect weather for an outing. It had been a month since the single *fraus'* last day trip. It offered something for each one to look forward to. Even Franny and Matilda had planned ahead this time and made extra chocolates each week leading up to tomorrow's trip so they'd both be free to join the others on this one this time. Rebekah had already stored the pretty little boxes in the propane refrigerator at her bakery shop so she could sell them while the others were away.

They had heard about the farmers' markets around the surrounding states, but one of the largest and oldest of them is located in St. Paul, Minnesota. It is over two and a half hours away by van each way from where they lived, but if you leave early enough you can actually make a whole day of it and return before it gets too late.

"It's a bucket list thing," Veronica explained to Ruth over coffee earlier that week. "You write down your wishes of things you want to see or do before you die and check them off as you accomplish each thing, see," she patiently told Ruth.

"Well, I'd like to see the Atlantic Ocean," Ruth told Veronica, "But I doubt if that wish will ever *kumm* true."

"Well, you *chust* have to work at it. It isn't magic. Why, you could go down to Pinecraft in Florida if you really wanted to. You could put an ad in *The Budget* and find out if anyone from around here is going next winter, say. I might even go with you! We'll take the train then," Veronica added slyly.

Veronica had written to Mrs. Dyck, their Mennonite driver, to see if she would be free to drive them the coming weekend. Mrs. Dyck had written back that she'd be happy to be their driver and that she loved going to the farmers' markets. Then she added at the end of her note,

"You know, the market closes at one o'clock. They all pack up and go home. We'd actually still have enough time to spend a few hours at the Como Zoo, too. It's been remodeled and it's a really nice place for the animals. I hated to see them in their old tiny cages back then, pacing back and forth. Now it's like they're living in the jungle, and we are in cages along all the paths. Let me know," she finished her letter.

Veronica had everyone's enthusiastic agreement to do both stops that day. Veronica suggested bringing a bag lunch to save on time and perhaps they could all eat supper out on the way home. Right at seven on the dot the van drove up to her kitchen door. The others were all in the van already: Hazel, Matilda, Franny, Ruth, Rachel, and Ruthie. Veronica made seven.

"Have *ya* all got your brown bag lunches?" she called as she wedged her way into the last remaining vacant seat. A volley of 'yeses' came back to her.

"Well, *gut.* Here goes nothing!" she said.

"This sure is a first for me," Rachel piped in first. "My first single *fraus'* adventure, my first St. Paul farmers' market, and my first trip to the Como Zoo."

"Mine too," Franny agreed. "I had all those chocolates to make last time you ladies were going out. A little planning ahead was all I needed this time."

Veronica located Hazel then and asked, "Hazel, how did you manage to get away?"

"Well," Hazel began. "She's got those *kinner* so well trained, she told me I absolutely had to get away for a day and made a list for each of the bigger *meedel* and *buwe* what they had to do for the day until I get back." And behind her hand, partially covering her mouth and lowering her voice, she added, "that *halsband chust* has to check up on those *kinner* and sit at the table and read his paper. She's even got him trained." They all howled at that.

Ruth and Veronica found themselves in a tiny cubicle at the huge hospital's genetics clinic. They'd looked around the waiting room when they first arrived and wondered that there were so many women and couples there. Were these problems so very common after all? They had received a letter earlier that week inviting them to come in to discuss the results of the bloodwork sent in from the medical practice near their community whom they were working with. The paperwork from the hospital where Veronica's baby had been born had also been sent to the clinic. "Do you think we'll really get our answers today? After...all this t...time? R... really?" Veronica stammered.

Ruth had suggested several months ago that they look into doing the study and try to get some concrete answers to

Veronica's questions. She wanted to know, if it could be discovered, once and for all, what her premature baby died from all those years ago, and secondly, what were the chances that other children she might have in the future would succumb to the same fate?

"I really can't say what they've found. What I do know, though, is that genetic science is discovering new things every day. It makes only five years ago look like the Dark Ages compared to today," Ruth offered.

"W...well, it will be a relief if I c-can, *ya* know, *chust* know one way or the other," Veronica concluded, though trembling inside.

"*Ya*. I'd want to learn all I could, I am thinking." Ruth thought a minute and then added, "You should know so you can move on, don't you think?"

"Exactly," Veronica agreed. The truth was that she wasn't one hundred percent sure she wanted to know. Not even fifty percent. It would definitely answer some questions she'd had for these many years. But it would also dictate her decisions about marriage, putting a final stamp on the prospect, one way or the other. Did she really want to do that? Was she sure? Is anybody really sure about such things? It could shape her entire future. Shouldn't she just trust the Lord in these things? Were we meant to dabble in so much science? Could that even be considered sinful? Maybe she should just let this all go....

Ruth knew how stressful this was for Veronica. She'd planned to take her out to lunch after the appointment hoping it would cheer her up. Whatever the final verdict on the tests was, she'd need some time to process this new information. Ruth could only imagine that if they were told she shouldn't plan on getting pregnant...ever, that her chances weren't good for having healthy babies, what effect would that devastating news have on Veronica? And conversely, if she were told that there were no apparent risks, what would that change? Would Veronica even believe it? How long would it take to actually absorb such good news? How would it affect her outlook? How she imagined the future could change, should that be the case.

CHAPTER 26

Nix the Celery

Dear Henry,

Greetings of love in our Dear Lord's Name!

I guess I am going to cut right to the point of this letter. I can't believe I am going to share this all with someone I haven't even met, yet. I owe you an explanation, I am thinking. I have started this letter a dozen times only to throw it in the stove.

I know I told you I wasn't interested in marrying again. I didn't think I could bear losing someone so close a second time. I'd be a terrible companion, not wanting to fall in love only to be hurt... resisting any kind of shared life only for it to be shattered. Then there was also the question of kinner. Burying one was too much to bear. I was sure all my future children were at risk of getting the same problems, or kumming so early, being premature, that they couldn't survive. I couldn't live through that again, and I certainly wasn't going to assume someone else would gladly take me on with those odds against me. They'd be stuck with a genuine basket case for sure. Not fair to you or anyone else.

Well, two things have happened that seem to point to Gott answering all my prayers. I am surprised. Shocked, really, after *harboring all these thoughts for all these years. Almost eight to be exact. He works in such mysterious ways and never how we think He would. Or should, ya know? Oh, ye of little faith!*

So, here's what's happened. We were out one day, the single fraus, and our driver, an older Mennonite woman, Mrs. Dyck, sort of a simple farm lady, said something that I chust *couldn't shake. She said she married again after her husband died suddenly, and she understood my hesitancy because I couldn't imagine being hurt again or whatever, but that only* Gott *is in charge of when people die, like the sparrow falling and He knows each one and what their time will be…well, I got to thinking about that. I could die first, or anything could happen and anticipating* Gott's *will is all wrong. If we were really like children, we could trust and put that out of our minds completely. Eight years is a long time to be stuck thinking I could control or avoid any of it. Made me think, for sure.*

And then, this midwife, Ruth, talked me into going to the university hospital that could do some blood tests and try to figure out what are my chances of only having kinner *with serious, inherited problems. So, it turns out they finally wrote back to us and had us* kumm *in to tell us what they found. They'd gotten the records from the hospital where I had my baby and were able to explain all of that to me. I guess I couldn't take in much at the time and* chust *didn't understand what all they told me way back then. It turns out she was growing pretty slowly and was premature because for some unexplained reason and I went into labor at seven months. Back then they didn't have the medications they have today that can often reverse labor and can even stop it, and with bedrest and such you can go to full term. Combined with that, they also hadn't had the newer medications they do now to treat the baby after it is born, with which they were only experimenting with back then.*

Two things happened. Boy, was this an eye-opener. They said the biggest risk to prematurity is that the baby's lungs haven't fully developed until after thirty-five weeks gestation. These newer meds are given to replace what your baby's lungs did not make before birth. It increases survival rates significantly.

The other problem was that they didn't know all that much about what oxygen levels to give premature babies. They used a respirator back then and guessed at how high to set the air. It was totally random. They really didn't have a clue. Now they know to mix it so babies aren't given one-hundred percent oxygen. Back then they chust didn't know. So, they told me, that too much pure oxygen can cause brain bleeds which is what happened. She was chust born at the wrong time. Her chances would have been so much better today, barely a decade later. They also said that they monitor mamms better prenatally, so they are able to help earlier before a bobbel kumms.

Then they got out the results from my blood tests and explained that there are absolutely no indications pointing to me carrying bad genes, or extra or missing chromosomes, or any hereditary factors. None at all. My chances of having healthy kinner in the future are exactly the same as anyone else. Who knew? And I fretted all those years. What a waste! "Worry ends where faith begins," they say. I am so much wiser now. I believe I could go into a marriage trusting Gott. I think I might...no, I probably would need reminding...maybe even daily. I chust feel that I cannot discount any of His leading any longer. I guess what I am saying is that I might be ready to meet you. Well, almost...and Rosie, too.

Friend Veronica

Ten days later...

Henry finished the milking that night, shared supper next door with his brother's family, and was back in the *dawdi haus* getting Rosie ready for bed. That's when he remembered the mail sitting on the table from earlier in the day. Addressing the plump baby on the bed, he finished pinning her diaper and scooped her up. "Let's go see what's in that letter, eh?" He cantered down the upstairs hallway while making little clicking sounds, jostling her for her favorite game they shared every night. She laughed out loud then, her deep baby voice rolling on and on as he continued galloping.

Henry perched her on one knee as he sat at the table and ripped open the envelope. He quickly scanned the letter, realizing this contained far more possibility than any of her previous letters ever had. Starting back at the beginning of the letter, he slowly read it again. Each line saw his grin widen, his furrowed brow relaxing.

He let out a long breath. "Wow. I didn't see that *kumming*. Did you Rosie? Whoa. I sure didn't expect that. Our prayers have been answered...I think. I am getting ahead of myself here. She still might not like me." Then looking down at Rosie who was busy attempting to reach for the saltshaker, he said, "But then, she won't be able to resist you...or then, she might be way worse than I've imagined. Well, time will tell, pumpkin." At that, he put the letter down on the table, and looked at Rosie. His eyebrows slowly moved upwards, and looking down at her, asked, "Clippity-clop?" to which she answered by bouncing up and down on his knee and waving her pudgy little arms. Standing up, he picked up the toddler then and cantered around the room singing that little ditty he often sang to her, "Who can tell what *Gott* can do? Who can tell what He'll do for you? In the na-ame of Jesus, Je-ee-sus, we have the vic-tor-y!"

To say that there was some serious rejoicing in a certain house in Milverton, Ontario the next day would be an understatement.

Henry Eicher sat to the right of his brother, Milo, at the long kitchen table with little Rosie in her highchair by his side. He waited until after the silent prayer to share the news he was fairly bursting with.

"She wrote," he could finally say. "And she wants me to visit. Can you believe it? After trying to put me off all these months. Almost a year."

His smile couldn't be any bigger. Rosie could sense her *dat* was happy and she followed suit by banging her little Peter Rabbit bowl on her highchair tray while the other children around the table sat with puzzled looks, wondering what it all meant.

As the serving dishes got passed around the table, Henry summed up the contents of Veronica's letter, carefully omitting the more personal aspects of it in deference to the children present.

"I still have to pinch myself. But then, I suppose we both might feel differently when we meet, but I am for certain looking forward to it. 'Time will tell' as they say."

His sister-in-law, Edith, spoke first. "When are you thinking of making the trip?"

He quickly answered, "As soon as possible. I'll write and let her know the dates, and get it cleared with my cousin, Jeremiah, down there so I can stay with theirs."

His brother spoke next. "We sure are happy for you. We'll pray for this trip. It's a big deal meeting like this."

"*Ya.* Sure is. I'll look into the Greyhound in the morning and write to her as soon as I can get it all straight," Henry replied.

Milo added, "We'll take care of Rose and all the chores *chust* fine. Don't worry about anything here, okay?"

They enjoyed a leisurely supper. Loaded potato soup topped the menu, filled with cheddar cheese, bacon, sour cream, and green onions. The chores had been done and all the children bathed earlier by the big wood cook stove. A couple of large canning kettles had been heated over the firebox and mixed with cold water from the gravity spigot in the kitchen. A galvanized grain/water trough had served as a bathtub all these years thus far, so they never thought to replace it quite yet, but the *kinner* were getting older and privacy would soon mean a proper tub space in the basement. They could still 'process' the children through the makeshift tub, sharing the water, adding more only as it cooled off. *Dat* would send the next one into the bath and *Mamm* would scrub every inch of skin, while kneeling by the tub, until she pronounced that one clean, despite all protests. Then *Dat* would get the next one ready and help them into the water, while grabbing a towel to rub down the clean little body by the warm stove, then sending them on their way to dress in the clean clothes *Mamm* had laid out in neat little piles in the great room on the chairs there. The process would be repeated until all were (literally) squeaky clean. Then their parents would carefully lift the tub together and dump the dirty water down the drain in the kitchen sink which ran out of the house and onto the orchard. The grain trough-cum-tub, being made of tin, made this job easier.

"I made dessert, y'all. Save your spoons," Edith said.

"What's the occasion anyway?" Milo asked craning his

neck back toward the stove. "You hardly ever make dessert unless it's a birthday or some such."

"Oh, you could say I had a hunch we'd be celebrating something tonight," was her coy answer. The fact was that she had picked up the mail earlier in the day and noticed the letter from the U.S. She hadn't seen a letter from Veronica in quite a while. She wondered at the time if things had cooled off with no letters coming. Edith prayed faithfully—for over a year now-- every night, for *Gott* to find a *frau* for Henry.

With that she passed down dessert bowls filled with warm peach cobbler topped with hot custard. The table became instantly silent then as they all enjoyed the rare treat.

"I'm not getting married *yet*," Henry protested between bites.

"*Gut* as...." Milo countered, his mouth half full.

"I've got enough peaches canned for that day too," Edith chuckled. Then as an afterthought she said, more to herself than to those at the table, "But we haven't planted any celery yet. Better get that going soon...."

Henry had heard her comment. "So what's with the celery thing, anyway?" he wanted to know. "They did that for my first marriage. This doesn't have to be the same big event too, does it? All that hoopla? Shoot! I mean *if* I even get married. *Chust* because it's a tradition doesn't mean it's a sacred tenant of our faith. Unnecessary if you ask me. Let's skip that part, why not? Besides, the Amish started that when they had the whole thing about the late fall being wedding season, after the last harvest when everyone wouldn't be so busy in the fields. By then all the *gut* vegetables had been canned and all that was left was kale and celery and a few Brussel sprouts. So they fancied up the celery with cream sauce and all. Silly how some ideas take off. Like a fad, and then get chiseled in stone. I say, forget the celery. We can use the propane coolers now and save other stuff from the garden longer anyway. I nix the celery. End of story," he concluded, his left fist hitting the table and making Rosie startle, and then laugh, as he picked up his spoon with his right hand to enjoy the dessert."

CHAPTER 27
New Beginnings

"When gratitude dwells in us, life becomes full of zest.

Dissatisfaction leaves us, to be replaced by a glorious sense of adventure

that makes our days like a song. Our daily work will glow,

and our lives will reflect God's beauty.

All things will come together in us to praise the Lord,

and the earth will be renewed and restored to Christ, to whom it belongs."

— *CATHERINE DOHERTY*

*D*o I even need a new adventure? she thought to herself as she reflected on the quote. *I am thinking I am too old for this. Maybe* chust *let me live this way, a quiet, plain life. I would be content. I don't need adventure. I don't need to 'glow,' whatever that means. But Your will, not mine be done*, she concluded, attempting to surrender the rest of her life into

His hands. Taking a deep breath, she squared her shoulders, while starting to list the chores she needed to attend to, though there was no hurry there.

Veronica lingered by the little calendar of inspirational sayings that she turned to a new page every morning. *All we can do is wonder at the greatness of* Gott, she thought to herself as she gazed at her favorite collection of thoughts by a woman she had never met and wouldn't now, until she went to heaven, too, Lord willing. *His workings are beyond anything we can imagine, eh?* she asked herself. Only yesterday she had heard back from Henry and since then had been trembling at the prospect now of actually meeting him. *What other surprises do You have up Your sleeve then,* Gott? *I can have healthy* kinner *after all, and I don't have to worry about losing all of them, either. I think Henry put it perfectly when he wrote that 'there is always risk when you love someone, but you leave that in His hands.' Hmph. I will always fret a bit I think, but you carry it together. I've been thinking all this time that it would all be up to me. Maybe a husband who is older and wiser would see our way through, together....*

All of a sudden, the thought struck her. *I should cut down that old swing in the front yard.*

The idea stunned her at first, actually. *I think it's about time. Am I ready? I guess it is as* gut *a time as any. Is one ever ready for change? It's a silly saying, but, 'there's no better time than the present...'*

Veronica brought her coffee mug to the kitchen table and sat down. An overcast day, threatening to rain. She could use it to read awhile, which she had not been able to do with the all the recent sunny days and all the work around the house. The garden was producing better than most years which kept her very busy just picking, pickling, canning and drying.

She canned everything she could: pickles, green beans, tomatoes, beets, carrots, ground cherries, peppers, even horseradish. She fermented sauerkraut to can later. She marinated a crock of thinly sliced eggplant rounds that would last all winter. With plenty of garlic, oregano and olive oil it made a great sandwich on fresh bread. She had even sent the Italian eggplant specialty to Maudie at *The Budget* for their upcoming new cookbook, too. All the garden would be harvested and put up by the time the apples were ready in the fall. That was a marathon in itself: Apple sauce, apple pie filling, apple butter, cider and apple jelly. And then dried *schnitz* apples for pies and cooking. During the Pandemic of 2020 she'd even discovered a recipe for *kimchi*, an Asian pickled delicacy using Napa cabbage, garlic, Thai peppers, canning salt, green onions, sugar, fresh ginger root, and fish sauce which, surprisingly, could be purchased at most grocery stores. One of the many benefits of it included boosting one's immune system—something that would greatly benefit one in these challenging times.

She thought of the garden as mission, something she could do to help others. A new baby in a busy family could always use some canned goods as would any going through hard times or illness. Farming isn't exactly always a lucrative business. Crops fail. Droughts happen. Too much rain can spoil a whole season's worth of work, too. Little gestures of support can mean a lot then. Giving away some of her own blessings would make her feel grateful, too. Sharing. She could do that.

She'd discovered solar-powered dehydrators earlier that year. She could now add fruit leather to the growing list of gift items she liked to make. She found packaged empty tea bags at a nearby health food co-op that she could fill with her dried mint, lemon balm, chocolate mint and spearmint, or any of the medicinal herbs she foraged on her walks. Wild red clover for recovering from childbirth, comfrey for poultices to heal open sores, wild ginseng for all sorts, yarrow for stomach problems, dandelion and golden seal root for cuts and warts, and black cohosh for menstrual cramps. She could fill the little bags, then sew the tops shut. They'd be stored in labeled jars to stay dry. She wanted to experiment with beef jerky, too though she had not found the time yet to research that one. Another day she would go to the library. Decorative jars of dried vegetables and beans would also make a pretty gift in a quart jar to make a soup supper later. The sky was the limit, she was finding, with what you could do with a dehydrator.

The herbs were fun to harvest, even after all of these years. Fragrant basil hung in bunches behind the wood stove on the drying rack she'd rigged up there, but not so close to the stovepipe that it would cook. There were also sprigs of oregano, and tarragon, and bundles of chives, swaths of parsley, dill, sage, and cilantro. *Yes, a gut day to finish these off or there'll be no room for picking more...*she thought to herself. *Breakfast first, though,* she told herself just as her pager set up its loud buzzing and vibrating, all while skittering across the table in fits and starts.

"Oh no!" she said out loud. "Now? Really?" she asked the thing as it came to life. Then she cornered and caught the little moving object.

She read the text there: "Be ready soon as" was all that was on the display screen.

"Oooof. I didn't see that one *kumming*..." she said aloud as she started shoveling in the corn meal *mosch*. Getting up from the table she scooped up the last mouthful, practically threw down the bowl with the spoon clattering onto the table and grabbed her coffee mug to run upstairs to dress.

Gut thing I have clean clothes ready, she reminded herself. *Wonder who it is? I should have been more prepared. I guess in this business you* chust *expect the unexpected, eh? Time to start praying. Well,* she began as she dressed, trying to compose herself, were that at all possible. *Do give Ruth wisdom, please Lord. Protect the* mamm *and* bobbel, *send your angels to surround this family, and be with us, please. Deliver this* bobbel *without any problems, please, PLEASE. In Jesus' Holy Name, Amen.* And then as an afterthought, *um, well, that will have to do Lord, I guess... but it's all in your Hands now, not ours.*

CHAPTER 28

The Visit

Dear Veronica,

Greetings of love in our Dear Lord's Name!

I've gotta say your letter brought me much joy. Even if we aren't meant for each other—and only Gott *knows that—I am so happy for you and your news from the tests. That's gotta be a huge relief, eh? Let me know if you are still at all interested in visiting. I mean, I could* kumm *there.*

It might be easier than you kumming *here with your canning and all, and now your midwife friend depending on you. On this end, my* bruder's *family will* chust *keep up the farm and all and watch Rosie besides. So I guess what I'm saying is, I'm free to visit.*

Please send me any proposed dates if this is a possibility for you.

Friend Henry

The day finally arrived. Henry was coming to visit. Was she even ready for this? Could she ever be? Had she wasted his time coming all this way from Canada by agreeing to meet him at long last? What if he didn't like her? What if he imagined her completely differently, and didn't feel interested when he actually met her? Would there be sparks? Or would she feel nothing at all?

She left the kitchen lintel and walked through the house where a gentle breeze wafted by her, the blue curtains waving their greetings. His cousin in the nearby district would be driving him over today. The bus had been scheduled to arrive there sometime yesterday morning. What if it had been late? Or canceled? Without a phone there was no way of knowing. Had she gone to all the trouble of cooking and cleaning for the past week for nothing? *Men usually don't even notice such things,* she told herself. *I hope his cousin will stay for dinner with us. I don't want to be stuck alone with him if the visit doesn't get off to a* gut *start. It would be a long drive back if he doesn't stay, and all for nothing*, she said to herself. Another thought appeared: *And I don't mind a chaperone, either. I'm not sure it would even be proper having him alone with me all day. Not exactly* Ordnung, *I'm thinking. And then pick him up later? That wouldn't make sense. I am sure the* bruder...*he'll stay to eat,* she reasoned to herself.

She wandered back out to the porch to wait. After only about ten minutes she saw a buggy far off making a sharp clip down the road, though it might just be someone else on their way to another farm. Then as it neared her mailbox it slowed. Yes, it was turning in. And yes, there was a *bruder* on the front bench-seat. Veronica held her breath. Standing up from the porch swing she worried that her knees wouldn't hold her up. Yes, it was him. Dressed for church Sunday by the looks of it. But he was alone. She hadn't expected that. Not at all.

A hasty prayer escaped her lips. *Oh help! Please. Show us the way. In Jesus' Name, please.*

CHAPTER 29

Wherever I Go...

As Henry descended from the buggy, he took the reins and led the horse up to the hitching post in the shade by the front of the house. He smiled, nodded toward her, then ever so slightly tipped his hat as he guided the horse into position. Veronica was baffled. *I thought his cousin or someone was bringing him. So, he borrowed the buggy and came all alone? Hmph. Well, now what do I do?* she asked and sent up another quick prayer. *He's tall. Looks pretty strong. I don't see any gray hairs,* she mumbled to herself. Then he turned around and leaned into the back of the buggy. *Oh no!* Veronica panicked. *Did he bring his suitcase, too, and think he was staying? No, buddy, this is not how this works. You can't think—*

And then Henry lifted little Rose out of the buggy. She looked over at Veronica and quickly shut her eyes, burying her head on her *dat's* shoulder. Smoothing down her dress he walked up to the porch. He had not uttered a word so far. Veronica was shocked. And delighted. And completely perplexed. What a strange man. Her heart skipped a beat. She soon realized she was standing there with her mouth still open and quickly shut it. They both stood there for what seemed like minutes. Finally, he took the bull by the horns and spoke first.

"Hi," was all he managed to say.

"Um, *ya*, hi," was all she could answer as she tried to take a few deep breaths.

"I borrowed the buggy. We slept at their place and headed out after that," he stated plainly.

"*Gut*" was all Veronica could say as they continued to size each other up. Then she came to her senses and added, "um, well...I have dinner made. Would you like to *kumm* in?"

As Henry began mounting the porch stairs, Veronica quickly opened the screen door and waved them inside.

"Uh," Henry began. "Maybe we ought to visit the outhouse first, like? It was a long ride for her—"

"Yes, sure," Veronica said as she turned to show them the way.

Finally, everyone was washed up and ready to take their places at the table.

"Oh, I forgot something. It's in the buggy," Henry said as he dashed back out the screen door, still holding Rosie who he was pretty sure would not want to be left alone quite yet with a stranger, as sweet as Veronica looked. Within minutes he strode up the stairs and back into the house, an old-fashioned, well-worn wooden highchair in one hand and Rosie still on his other arm, though this time she was hugging a much-loved faceless Amish doll who was also wearing a dear little rose-colored dress with a matching pinafore and tiny black bonnet.

Veronica's heart melted. Was this what Henry had calculated all along? Why hadn't she thought of this possibility? Well, he sure surprised her. That was certain. "What is your dolly's name?" she asked in Pennsylvania Dutch, knowing full well that Rosie wouldn't learn English until she started school.

The beautiful child answered quite clearly. "Rosemary." Then Henry set her down on her feet, brushing her hem down once again.

And again in *Deutch* Veronica answered her. "That's a lovely name. And you are Rose?"

The little girl lifted her chin then, and with a very decided nod walked over to her highchair.

Henry lifted her up and settled her in the chair and then quickly inhaled, "Um, I forgot to bring a bib...."

"Oh, no problem. I'll grab a tea towel," she said, practically tripping over her own feet as she turned and opened a drawer at the counter while Henry sat down. Then again Veronica addressed Rose. "It is okay if I put on your bib?"

Again, the child gave a clear nod, this time adding a tiny smile. Again, Veronica felt her heart squeeze in her chest.

"I'll, uh, get...um, everything out," she stammered, as she realized this man had rendered her completely speechless. She was so unprepared for her reaction. To him. To Rosie.

He appeared just as *ferhoodled*. "Ah...is there anything I can, um, do? To, *ya* know...bring over?"

"No, I think I've got everything, *ya* know, under control," she answered and then to herself, *I don't have anything under control, actually. No, not a blesséd thing....*

She scurried over to the pie then off to the side of the room and added a plastic child's dish to the stack there waiting for dessert. Veronica turned to the hutch cupboard where the mugs were lined up and pulled down the blue speckled tin cup she'd gotten for Christmas all those years ago, so proud to have a cup just like Laura's and Mary's. Pausing for a moment with the little enamel mug in her hands she marveled that, here she was, with the very cup she'd saved all these years and was now using for sweet

Rosie. *Wonders never cease,* she pondered. Snapping back to the present, she poured in about an inch of camel milk from the little jar in the ice chest and was about to put it down in front of Rosie when Henry reached out to take it. "I didn't tell you but she's allergic to dairy so we're trying to do without," he explained. Veronica blinked, taking back the mug.

"So am I. Huh. Who would have thought? Well, so this is actually camel milk. It is lactose-free," she explained. "Have you tried giving it to her?" she asked.

"Why, no. Camel milk, you say. Really?" Henry asked incredulously and then added, "we usually give her *chust* goat milk."

"Well," Veronica explained. "This is *gut* too, for that, I mean. There's an Amish-owned dairy set up in Missouri recently. The camels give about three gallons a day and they ship it all over the states now."

"Well, okay," Henry said. "That's pretty amazing. And you say it's Amish-owned? Huh. Whatever next?"

"I know," Veronica commiserated as she continued to set serving dishes on the table. Finally, she sat down, smiling at Rose who was being so quiet while just watching her. She was rewarded by a shy dip of the child's head and again that cheeky little smile. Veronica placed her hands under the table and gave an almost imperceptible nod to Henry, who understood the invitation to lead the silent grace.

"Patties down," he said, looking at Rose who instantly slid her hands under her highchair tray and shut her eyes which popped open the second Henry cleared his throat, signaling the end of the prayer.

Veronica surprised herself then as the thought popped into her head: *Well, I guess I got that chaperone I'd wished for. So adorable, eh?*

"Here, why don't you start with the meat," she said as she indicated the dish in front of him.

"*Denki*," he replied taking the platter. "This all looks so *wunderbar-gut*. You didn't have to go to so much fuss for us, though," he added, passing the plate back.

"*Ach!* No fuss. I've been looking forward to this, *ya* know," she explained. "I like to cook and, well, you don't do so much *chust* for one, do you?"

"No, I don't figure you do. What are these?" Henry asked, taking a roll from the basket between them.

"That's *zupha*. It comes from the Swiss Amish. I saw it in Maudie's recipes in *The Budget* awhile back. They're easy enough to whip up," she said.

"*Ya*, Becky tried those recipes out, too. Most were pretty *gut*. Some were flops, I have to admit," Henry added with a laugh.

"You get *The Budget* in Canada then?" she wanted to know.

"*Ya*. It goes all over North *and* South America," he informed her.

"Huh. I didn't realize that," she said.

"And what is this?" Henry asked, pointing to a Corning Ware dish.

"That's potato and dumplings. With sour cream sauce," she explained.

"And that?" he continued.

"Ah, that one is called 'Shipwreck.' Also from Maudie."

"Well, I *chust* never saw some of these. Being way off in Canada, we are behind you in *chust* about everything, I reckon," he surmised.

Changing the subject Veronica asked Henry, "So, how old is Rosie?"

The child answered for him, holding up three fingers and tried to say, 'three' with her mouth full.

"So, not school yet for another year then, *liebling?*" Veronica asked.

Another decisive nod from Rosie answered the question. Veronica chuckled.

"How did you get so smart, anyway?" Veronica ventured.

They both laughed then when Rosie simply pointed to her *dat,* with her mouth full.

"Well, I gotta say it was quite a surprise when you got her out of the buggy. I wouldn't have guessed you'd do that, *ya* know. Bring her with you. Such a surprise," Veronica admitted.

"I, uh, hadn't planned on it either, truth be told. It didn't occur to me till the day before the trip and I realized my sister-in-law has been under the weather lately and my *bruder* told me they're expecting again and I'd planned on leaving Rosie with them, but then I thought the last thing Edith needed was more *kinner,*" he explained.

"Well, that explains a lot. I was thinking you'd know I'd fall for her, and you'd have a shoe in, kind of. I'm sorry I thought you'd done it to trick me somehow," Veronica confessed.

"Oh, no. I am so sorry. I wouldn't think that. Sorry you got that impression. No, it wasn't calculated, not in the least," he apologized.

"Well, whether you planned it or not, I think she is precious. She has stolen my heart I have to admit."

"I am glad," Henry said, gazing at Veronica for a long moment. "She is all that keeps me going some days. I never thought I'd be in this spot, in my whole life, *ya* know? A widower," Henry said as he put down his fork and scooped up some more dumplings and potatoes into Rosie's dish.

"Me either. Life is *chust* full of surprises, *eh?*" she commiserated.

"I dunno. Seems like some *chust* get more surprises than others, though. Why is that?" Henry asked, looking up at Veronica.

"Don't ask me. I don't understand any of it. I guess I also see *chust* enough goodness perhaps, to make it possible to want to go on living. Maybe?" she asked. Henry nodded. Changing the subject, as impossible as it would be to answer such ponderous questions, he switched back to the wonderful dinner before them.

"I gotta thank you, though, for this meal. It's really gut!" He praised her.

"Like I said, I enjoy cooking,"

"And I sure like that you like cooking. So does Rosie," he said while watching the little girl carefully picking up one pea at a time with her left hand and delicately placing it on the spoon she was holding in her right before popping it in her mouth. She had been listening to the whole conversation and at the mention of her name, again nodded. Henry looked at Veronica then and she looked at him. No words were needed. They both knew. This had been the plan from all Eternity. *His* plan for them. According to the world, it would seem folly. But to those that have embraced this path less trod, it couldn't be more clear. Their gazing was interrupted by a tiny voice then. "More...please." Rosie looked up at both of them and smiled. She seemed to know, too.

That night as she was saying her prayers on her knees by the bed, her head bowed, Veronica was at a loss for words, marveling instead at God's infinite wisdom and mercy. How could He possibly look out for each and every little person in the whole universe, much less all the animals, even a tiny sparrow? How could He direct her life, as insignificant as she was, even to the point of finding a new friend to share her life with? It positively boggled her mind how He can be so very great and keep the immeasurable oceans and all the skies and stars and cosmos, the earth and all its creatures living out their time in the entire universe while still caring that she is growing in wisdom and in faith. *It is all too great for me,* she concluded silently. *The depth and width and breath of all creation bows before Him,* she remembered from the Psalms. And then aloud, "Wherever *I* go, there *YOU* are...."

The End

Coming Soon
The Amish Veronica Book 2
You Have Ravished My Heart

———————————

Don't miss out on your next favorite book!

Join the Satin Romance mailing list
www.satinromance.com/mail.html

"God speaks quietly, very quietly but He does speak, and He will make known to you what He wants you to do."

— CATHERINE DOHERTY

Acknowledgments

I have given birth to a series of books full of true stories and memories gathered from a lifetime of amazing encounters with other cultures and diverse peoples.

I owe a great debt to the mothers and babies I have had the privilege of serving for so many years and all I learned from each one: Amish *mamms*, Hutterite *mutters*, Hmong *nias*, Vietnamese, Somali, Ethiopian, Native American, and all the other brave women I have met.

I also owe a great debt of gratitude to WOW (Women of Words) and NLW/RWA (Northern Lights Writers/ Minnesota chapter of Romance Writers of America,) and Patricia Morris (past president of MIPA, Minnesota Independent Publishers Association,) and Phyllis Moore, all author-friends who have so unselfishly shared their wisdom and experience of the writing and publishing world with me. I couldn't have done this without each one of you!

And Janet Marchant, librarian, beta reader extraordinaire, and a dear friend, thanks for her advice, suggestions and expertise in all things books. Thank you!

I want to especially thank Nancy Schumacher and her brilliant team at Melange Books who were my midwives and doulas throughout the birthing of my books.

Of course, I can't end without expressing my eternal gratitude to my dearest husband of 47 years, David, and my children, Abraham, Isaac, Ruth, Rachel, and HRuthh Rose for their undying love, encouragement and support no matter how *ferhoodled* mother's latest creation appears to be.

Appendix

MORE READING...

- *Blackboard Bulletin* is a monthly Amish magazine for Old Order teachers produced by Pathway Publishers, in Aylmer, Ontario.
- *The Budget.* A weekly correspondent newspaper that includes reports from scribes in Amish communities across the nation. It is published in Sugarcreek, Ohio. The first edition came out in 1890.
- *The Connection* is a monthly glossy magazine whose purpose is "connecting our Amish communities." It features Amish columnists from Indiana, Iowa, Kentucky, Michigan, Missouri, Ohio, and Pennsylvania, who write about farming, cooking, health practices, life experiences, and spiritual reflections. It comes out of Topeka, Indiana.
- *The Diary* is another monthly correspondent magazine with reports from scribes in many

Amish settlements as well as sections on weddings, births, deaths, and accidents and other special columns. It is printed and available from Kirkwood, Pennsylvania.

- *Family Life.* A monthly Amish family and community magazine with articles, poetry, recipes, and children's stories. It is also published by Pathway Publishers, in Aylmer, Ontario, Canada.

- *Farming Magazine.* A quarterly magazine that focuses on small-scale farming, it comes out of Hope, OH.

- *The Ladies' Journal* is a bimonthly glossy-cover woman's magazine featuring regular columns on motherhood, marriage, women's health, and homemaking. The writers come from a variety of Plain backgrounds, but the editor is Old Order Amish. It hails from Loysville, Pennsylvania.

- *Life's Special Sunbeams.* A monthly magazine featuring stories by Amish parents of special needs children, as well as a regular questions-and-answers column and a Teacher's Reflections section. Also available in a Braille edition. This publisher is located in New Holland, Pennsylvania.

- *Little Red Hen News.* A quarterly woman's magazine written and edited by Amish women with some Old Order Mennonite women contributors. It features short articles—often in the form of letters from readers—on household tips, gardening, and childrearing, as well as short stories and poetry. It is produced in Marion, Kentucky.

- *Pilgrim's Pathway* is a New Order Amish bimonthly publication promoting biblical standards for home, church, and school. It comes from Heritage Publishers, in Sugarcreek, Ohio.
- *Plain Communities Business Exchange.* A monthly newspaper for Old Order businesses with articles, ads, and a calendar of business-related events, from Millersburg, Pennsylvania.
- *Plain Interests.* A monthly magazine featuring short articles on farming, health practices, life experiences, and spiritual reflections. Its perspective is slanted toward organic farming and alternative medicine. Most writers are Amish, but Old Order Mennonites write occasionally. There is also a "Letters to the Editor" section, where readers can respond to articles. This magazine comes from Millersburg, Ohio.
- *Single Symphony Magazine* – from Thorp, Wisconsin. Written and published by Plain single men and women.
- *Truck Patch News.* Monthly newsletter with articles and advertisements of help and interest for the Amish produce farmer. It comes from Mt. Hope, Ohio.
- *Young Companion.* A monthly magazine for children and teens comes out of Aylmer, Ontario, Canada.

THANK YOU FOR READING

Did you enjoy this book?

We invite you to leave a review at your favorite book site, such as Goodreads, Amazon, Barnes & Noble, etc.

DID YOU KNOW THAT LEAVING A REVIEW...

- Helps other readers find books they may enjoy.
- Gives you a chance to let your voice be heard.
- Gives authors recognition for their hard work.
- Doesn't have to be long. A sentence or two about why you liked the book will do.

About the Author

Midwife-turned-author, Stephanie Schwartz seems to swim seamlessly through cultures, religions, superstitions, raw fear and ecstasy to the first breath of a new baby. She knows how birth works and invites her readers to join her, taking us on a tour to the innermost workings of another world while giving us a rare, intimate glimpse into her daily life. She has five children scattered around the world, grandchildren, and over a thousand babies she calls her own. After writing three books on birth, (published under her married name, Sorensen) and then retiring as a midwife, began her foray into fiction. Thanks to the Pandemic she was able to produce the four novels in the Amish Nurse Series.

facebook.com/authorstephanieschwartz

newamishromance@yahoo.com

Also by Stephanie Schwartz

The Amish Nurse Series
Worry Ends Where Faith Begins
Time Will Tell
Playing on the Outhouse Roof
The Pearl of Great Price

The Amish Veronica Series
Wherever You Go There You Are
You Have Ravished My Heart

Made in the USA
Columbia, SC
09 January 2025

51488059R10136